THE
MOLE

A Dylan Kane Thriller

Also by J. Robert Kennedy

James Acton Thrillers

The Protocol
Brass Monkey
Broken Dove
The Templar's Relic
Flags of Sin
The Arab Fall
The Circle of Eight
The Venice Code
Pompeii's Ghosts
Amazon Burning
The Riddle
Blood Relics

Sins of the Titanic
Saint Peter's Soldiers
The Thirteenth Legion
Raging Sun
Wages of Sin
Wrath of the Gods
The Templar's Revenge
The Nazi's Engineer
Atlantis Lost
The Cylon Curse
The Viking Deception
Keepers of the Lost Ark
The Tomb of Genghis Khan

The Manila Deception
The Fourth Bible
Embassy of the Empire
Armageddon
No Good Deed
The Last Soviet
Lake of Bones
Fatal Reunion
The Resurrection Tablet
The Antarctica Incident
The Ghosts of Paris
No More Secrets

Dylan Kane Thrillers

Rogue Operator
Containment Failure
Cold Warriors
Death to America
Black Widow

The Agenda
Retribution
State Sanctioned
Extraordinary Rendition

Red Eagle
The Messenger
The Defector
The Mole
The Arsenal

Just Jack Thrillers
You Don't Know Jack

Zander Varga, Vampire Detective
The Turned

Templar Detective Thrillers

The Templar Detective
The Parisian Adulteress
The Sergeant's Secret

The Unholy Exorcist
The Code Breaker

The Black Scourge
The Lost Children
The Satanic Whisper

Kriminalinspektor Wolfgang Vogel Mysteries
The Colonel's Wife   Sins of the Child

Delta Force Unleashed Thrillers

Payback
Infidels
The Lazarus Moment

Kill Chain
Forgotten
The Cuban Incident

Rampage
Inside the Wire
Charlie Foxtrot

Detective Shakespeare Mysteries

Depraved Difference   Tick Tock   The Redeemer

THE

MOLE

A Dylan Kane Thriller

J. ROBERT KENNEDY

UNDERMILL
PRESS

Copyright ©2022 J. Robert Kennedy

ISBN: 9781990418501

First Edition

For Stephen "tWitch" Boss.

May your death inspire those in pain to seek the help they so desperately need.

THE
MOLE

A Dylan Kane Thriller

"The East is rising and the West is declining."

Chinese President Xi Jinping

"The biggest source of chaos in the present-day world is the United States…The United States is the biggest threat to our country's development and security."

Chinese President Xi Jinping
February 2021

PREFACE

On October 22, 2022, during the Chinese Communist Party Congress, something unprecedented happened. Caught on camera, Hu Jintao, the 79-year-old former president of the communist regime, was physically escorted from the meeting by men who lifted him out of his chair.

What was telling was the reaction of the current president, Xi Jinping, who essentially ignored his predecessor, even though the man was clearly confused as to what was going on.

The Party provided no explanation. Was this a preemptive move by the Chinese president to prevent Hu from speaking against the unprecedented third term Xi was about to be granted by a coopted party?

And if the Chinese president were willing to make such a public move against an opponent, what else might he be willing to do to cement his permanent grip on power?

Tong Residence

Falls Church, Virginia

"You have got to be kidding me!"

CIA Senior Analyst Sonya Tong slammed her fist into the steering wheel. She pressed the button to start the engine once again. It turned over but failed to catch. "Stupid! Stupid! Stupid!" she repeated as both fists beat the steering wheel, punctuating each enraged outburst. It was cold out, but it was by no means Antarctic cold. A two-year-old car should have no problem starting.

It wasn't, after all, a notorious British sports car with a famously faulty electrical system.

She didn't have time for this shit. She was already running behind as it was, and this would make her uncharacteristically late. She was scheduled to work an op in an hour. One of their top operatives, CIA Operations Officer Dylan Kane, was inserting into China, and she had to be there. She gave the engine one more try, slammed her fist one more time, then called the toll-free number on the roadside assistance sticker in the upper left-hand corner of her windshield. She arranged for a tow, then grabbed her purse and bag, rushing down the driveway of her still new-to-her home and toward the bus stop.

She rarely took the bus. She could count on one hand how many times she had in this neighborhood, and wasn't familiar with the schedule, though she was certain the buses were at least half an hour apart. The chirp of airbrakes then the roar of an engine had her cursing and picking up speed as the bus she couldn't see approached from around the corner. The last 200 yards were on a slight incline and her shins burned. She did forty minutes on the treadmill every day, but that was in comfortable clothes with running shoes and at an incline far less than this.

She spotted the bus stop, three people at it already edging to the curb. "Hold the bus!" she shouted.

A man in a business suit turned, the other two ignoring her. He smiled and gave her a wave. "I've got you!"

She flashed him a smile but kept up her pace as the bus came into sight. Several people disembarked from the rear door as those waiting boarded at the front, the man standing in the door, one foot still on the curb, saying something to the driver.

She rounded the corner and eased up. "Thank you so much," she gasped, and he smiled at her.

"No problem. Maybe one day you'll return the favor."

She stepped onto the bus. "Absolutely, though hopefully my car doesn't break down again anytime soon." She stepped to the fare box then tossed her head back, groaning. "I don't think I have any change. Who uses cash anymore?"

The man chuckled and tapped his SmarTrip pass twice. "I'll take care of her," he told the driver.

"It's your four-twenty-five."

Tong's shoulders slumped as she turned to the man. "Oh, thank you so much." The bus started up and she shuffled down the aisle, taking an empty seat. She smiled up at the man. "Please, join me."

"I thought you'd never ask."

It was then that she finally noticed how strikingly handsome the man was, his smile so genuine, so inviting, that she caught herself staring. She snapped out of it with a flinch and retrieved her wallet from her bag. "You have to let me pay you," she said as she flipped open her wallet, finding only large bills. "I don't suppose you can break a twenty?"

He laughed. "Forget the money. How about you give me your number? Maybe we can go for coffee sometime?"

Her cheeks flushed and a tingle raced through her body. She was certain this was the first time a man had ever asked her out in her life. Well, that couldn't be true. She had been on dates before, though most of those were blind, arranged through family or friends. She had certainly never been asked out by a stranger. There had always been some previous connection.

"Should I take your silence as a no?"

She flinched again, giggling, immediately horrified at the sound.

Did you just giggle? What are you? Twelve?

"No. I mean, no, you shouldn't interpret it as a no."

"So then, it's a yes?" The smile broadened, revealing a perfect set of teeth, the twinkle in his hazel eyes declaring he was genuinely pleased.

"Yes. I mean, yes, it's a yes."

He laughed. It was a good laugh, a laugh she could enjoy without cringing. The bus came to a halt as he pulled out his phone. "Why don't you give me your number and I'll text you?"

She gave him her number and he entered it when there was a shout from the front of the bus. Two gunshots rang out and passengers screamed as a crazed man burst up the steps, a handgun extended in front of him. He fired two more rounds into the driver then swung his weapon toward the commuters.

Tong stared ahead, her eyes fixated on the barrel of the weapon, unable to see anything else. The gunman shouted something, what, she couldn't hear above the roar in her ears.

Breathe.

She sucked in a breath, inhaling deeply, her world snapping back into focus, and she raised her eyes to see the gunman staring directly at her.

"Stop following me!" he screamed, then the muzzle flashed. Agony slammed into her shoulder and she slumped in her seat as the pain overwhelmed her. Her seatmate shouted something, and as she drifted into unconsciousness, she added yet another regret to a long list.

I never even got his name.

Operations Center 2, CIA Headquarters

Langley, Virginia

CIA Analyst Supervisor Chris Leroux entered the operations center and his eyebrows rose at Sonya Tong's empty chair. He rarely beat her in. "Morning, everyone," he said as he took his position at his station in the heart of the state-of-the-art room. The half-dozen of his team already there replied, pleasantries exchanged. His cellphone rang and he picked it up off the desk, his eyes narrowing at the call display.

Langley Memorial Hospital.

His chest tightened for a moment before he remembered that his girlfriend was on an op in Europe and his best friend Kane was why they were all here today. He took the call. "Hello?"

"Hello. This is Nurse Cummings from Langley Memorial. Am I speaking to Chris Leroux?"

"You are." His eyes drifted to the empty chair of Tong.

"You're listed as the emergency contact for Sonya Tong."

He shot to his feet. "Is she all right?"

The entire room stopped what they were doing at the panic in his voice.

"She's in surgery right now. I don't have a prognosis yet."

"What happened?" asked Leroux as he began packing up his gear.

"I only know a few of the details. Apparently, there was an incident on a bus this morning and she was shot. I don't know anything beyond that. Will you be attending?"

"Yes, of course. I'll be there as soon as I can."

"You should notify her family if she has any, just in case."

"It's that bad?"

There was a pause. "Turn on the news. I'll let you go now, sir. When you get here, come to the ICU nursing station."

"All right. I understand." He ended the call. "Bring up the local news."

Randy Child, their tech wunderkind, leaned toward his keyboard. "Any particular station?"

"All of them." His voice cracked at the thought of losing Tong. He had worked with her for years. She was a good friend, and he was well aware she had feelings for him and that she was all alone. He had to be by her side.

Several stations appeared on the massive displays arcing across the front of the room, and he pointed at one showing a breaking news alert. "Bring that one up."

Child complied, the feed expanding to fill the entire display, the audio piping in through the overhead speakers.

"—just joining us, there's been a mass shooting on a Fairfax Connector bus in Falls Church, Virginia. Five people are dead and three people are wounded, one critically. Authorities report an unidentified female passenger is in surgery now, clinging to life. Witnesses stated the gunman boarded the bus, shouting about being followed. He shot the bus driver then a female passenger, then several others before finally being taken down by an unnamed passenger. The gunman is dead—"

Leroux waved his fingers in front of his throat and Child muted the broadcast. Leroux faced his team. "The passenger clinging to life is…" He squeezed his eyes shut, drawing a deep breath. "It's Sonya." Gasps filled the room as he wagged his phone. "I just got a call from the hospital. I'm going there now."

Marc Therrien, one of the senior analysts, cleared his throat. "Um, what about the op, boss?"

Leroux cursed, their entire purpose for being here forgotten. "You're right. Marc, you're in charge. I'm going to go talk to the Chief, see if we can swap off to another team. I'll check and see if Avril's team can take over." He headed for the door and Child rose.

"Hey, boss."

Leroux turned to see the young man's eyes red and glistening. "Keep us posted."

Leroux looked at the others, concern on all their faces. They were family, and he was the head of it, and it was his job to bring them comfort. He stopped at the doorway. "As soon as I know something I'll let you know. But we all know and love…" His voice cracked at the word, triggering tears in some of those seeking strength from him. He sniffed hard. "We all know and love her. She's a fighter. If anybody can make it through this, it's her. Let's just all pray. I'm going to go talk to the Chief and see if we can get the op reassigned, or at least a new Control Actual in here. If any of you feel you can't work, let Marc know." He turned to Therrien. "That goes for you too."

Marc gave a thankful smile. "I'll be all right, boss. You go do what you need to do."

Leroux gave a curt nod then headed out the door and across the corridor to the standby ops center, a team always assigned to it for situations just like this. He entered and was surprised to see David Epps standing at the Control station instead of Avril Casey. "What are you doing here? I thought Avril was on duty."

Epps gave him a look. "Well, good morning to you too." He stopped, his eyes narrowing. "What's wrong?" The concern in Epps' voice was sincere, personal, not just professional.

Leroux dragged a knuckle across his eyelid, wiping away a tear. "Sonya's been shot."

A collective gasp erupted from the room, and Epps rushed from his station, joining Leroux by the door. "Is she going to be all right?"

Leroux squeezed his eyes shut. "I don't know. I'm heading to the hospital now, but I'm going to see the Chief first."

"You need us to take over?"

"Can you?"

"Absolutely, that's what we're here for."

"Good. I'll let the Chief know what's going on." Leroux checked his watch. "Dylan is inserting in about half an hour. Integrate in my team

that are still up for working. They're fully briefed. I left Marc in charge."
He opened the door and paused. "Where's Avril?"

Epps shrugged. "Nobody can reach her. I got called in at four this morning to cover for her. When I do see her, my wife's asked me to pass a few choice words on to her."

Leroux wanted to laugh, but it just wasn't in him.

Epps flicked his fingers at the door. "Go. Your op is in good hands."

Leroux left the room, feeling a little better as Epps began barking orders. The last thing any of them would want, especially Tong, was for Kane to be left hanging when he was entering hostile territory.

Casey Residence

Pimmit Hills, Virginia

"Help me."

Avril Casey was so weak she couldn't be certain the mouthed words had any sound behind them. The doorbell rang again and a fist pounded, the sound carrying up the stairs and into the bathroom. "Help me," she repeated, and this time she was certain she made a sound, but it was barely a murmur.

No one was hearing her.

She forced her eyes open, struggling to make sense of what was happening. Her brain barely registered that she was in her tub, water up to her neck, yet it wasn't water. It was pink, almost red. What was going on? She shivered, the water cold. How had she gotten here? She struggled to pierce the fog clouding her mind. She had no recollection of taking a bath, yet she obviously had. She must have fallen asleep for the water to be so cold. Could that be why she was weak? A mild form of hypothermia?

The doorbell continued to ring, rapidly now, the hammering nearly constant. She glanced over to see sunlight pouring through the window. It was daytime. She was supposed to have been at work for the night shift. She was scheduled as Control Actual for the backup ops center. It must be somebody from the CIA sent to check on her. She struggled to get out of the bath but collapsed.

"Help me." Again, barely a murmur. She had to get out of here, yet the cold water was sapping her of her strength and weighing her down. And why was it red? She closed her eyes and prayed to God for strength, and he granted it to her. Just a little bit, just enough for her to reach behind her and press the drain stopper. It popped up and she could hear the water rapidly flow out of the tub, the waterline receding slowly, a red ring marking where it had obviously sat for hours.

Why is it red?

The water continued to drop, revealing her knees and chest, then finally her entire body. She raised her hand to grip the edge of the tub then gasped. There were long deep slits in her left wrist, blood slowly oozing from the cuts. She pulled her other arm from behind her back and a lump formed in her throat when she found her other wrist sliced open as well.

What's happening?

Her wrists were slit. She was in a tub that likely held warm water to stimulate blood flow when she first climbed in. She had obviously attempted to commit suicide, but why? She couldn't remember. She attempted to lift her arm one more time to pull herself out of the tub, but it wouldn't move. The answer to her prayers had given her enough energy only to reveal to her the truth and nothing more.

She wouldn't be saving herself today.

And if she had indeed committed the ultimate sin of killing herself, she didn't deserve to be saved. Yet that couldn't be what had happened. She was happy. She had a great career, people she liked and who liked her at the office, friends, a nice home, and a boyfriend who loved her.

Her barely beating heart skipped a precious beat at the thought of her boyfriend, a sense of foreboding washing through her. He had something to do with this. She knew it, but she couldn't be sure what. She just sensed fear when she thought of him. But why? Why would she fear the man she loved?

The laptop.

Her eyes shot wide with a final burst of energy as everything came flooding back. Dinner, making love, having a shower, leaving it running for him, discovering him on her CIA laptop, logged into the system with a password he couldn't possibly know, him grabbing her then spraying her face with something.

And then nothing.

Until now.

As the door was kicked open downstairs, she exhaled her final breath, comforted by the fact she hadn't committed suicide but had been murdered, though dismayed the man she thought loved her had used her because of her position. What terrified her wasn't what was to come, but what his betrayal might mean for the operatives whose lives she held in her hands every day. Her entire body relaxed as her mind faded to black, her problems now the responsibility of the living.

I'm ready, God.

Brooklyn Tanner shoved the door aside, having arrived only a moment ago, a Langley staffer sent to check on Avril Casey calling in that she couldn't reach the analyst supervisor, despite the fact her car was in the driveway. Echo Team, a special forces team under the direction of the CIA but seconded to Homeland Security so they could operate on American soil, had been dispatched, and she didn't bother wasting time with pleasantries like knocking.

Her second-in-command, Michael Lyons, had used a battering ram to break down the door. She cleared the living room, heading toward the kitchen as Lyons broke right. "Avril, can you hear me? Are you here?" There was no response. As she entered the kitchen, she noticed everything was spotless, not a thing out of place, not a smudge anywhere. She indicated the door to the basement and Lyons headed down the steps.

"Holy shit, Tanner! Second floor!" shouted Chris Morrissette.

"Clear!" announced Lyons from the basement as she headed for the stairs to the second floor. She took them two at a time to find the other two team members standing outside the bathroom door.

"What is it?"

Morrissette shook his head. "Not good."

She stepped into the bathroom and cursed. Casey was in the tub, the water drained, a red ring around the top suggesting it had been full at one point. Her wrists were slit, her body ghostly pale. She stepped forward, removing a glove, then took a knee, checking for a pulse. She cursed again. Nothing. There was a scream behind her and she spun to see the staffer standing there, a hand slapped over her mouth, her eyes wide.

Tanner frowned. "Get her out of here. And call this in."

"Who?" asked Morrissette.

"Call the Chief. Let him decide how he wants to get the locals involved."

Lyons poked his head inside. "Holy shit!"

Morrissette grunted. "That's what I said. I don't think I've ever seen anything like this before."

Lyons agreed. He reached in and picked up a piece of paper lying on the vanity counter. "Suicide note."

"What's it say?" asked Tanner.

Lyons read it. "I'm sorry for what I've done. The guilt of it is tearing me apart and I can't go on knowing I've hurt the ones who put their trust in me. Avril." He flipped the page around, holding it up so she could see it. "Typed."

Tanner cocked an eyebrow. "Typed? She actually typed then printed off her suicide note? I thought they were usually handwritten?"

Lyons shrugged. "No idea. You'd have to ask Columbo."

"Who?"

"Some TV detective my father likes to watch. Seventies, I think."

Tanner grunted. "I wasn't even born." She pointed at the countertop. "Put that back where you found it. Take a photo of it. Send it to the Chief and we'll await instructions. Right now, secure the house. Standard protocol. Sweep for any electronic surveillance, secure any Agency property. The paperwork on this one isn't going to be fun."

Director Morrison's Office, CIA Headquarters

Langley, Virginia

"Is he in?"

National Clandestine Service Chief Leif Morrison's assistant nodded at Leroux. "Yes, but he's on a call."

Leroux didn't hear the words. Between his conversation with Epps and reaching his boss' office, he had created a completely revised history of his life where Sherrie hadn't entered it and he and Tong were instead dating, deeply in love with each other, blissfully happy. It was now no longer a colleague fighting for her life, but the woman he was supposed to marry.

He opened the door to Morrison's inner office.

"Chris, what are you doing?" exclaimed the assistant behind him, but again, her words went ignored.

Morrison sat behind his desk, his phone pressed to his ear. He didn't appear surprised at Leroux bursting in, instead holding up a finger then pointing at an empty chair. Leroux opened his mouth to interrupt when the Chief gave him a look that had him snapping back to reality. Morrison's assistant was waved off and she closed the door as Leroux dropped into a chair, his foot tapping impatiently.

"I'll have the local authorities notified. We want to do this by the book, but take photos of everything before the locals get there. Have you secured her equipment?... Good. Put that in your vehicle immediately...No, leave the letter...I'll be sending a liaison officer over. Keep the scene secure, but as soon as the locals arrive, surrender control to them...Very well." Morrison hung up the phone and sighed heavily. He regarded Leroux then his eyes narrowed. "What's wrong?"

Leroux rapid fired the response. "Sonya's been shot. She's in surgery. I need to go to the hospital. I need to stand my team down. Dylan's on an op. He's inserting at the top of the hour." He pinched the bridge of his nose, squeezing his eyes shut as he struggled to maintain control. Morrison's chair creaked and a moment later a gentle hand was on Leroux's shoulder.

"Take a breath, son."

Leroux gasped in a lungful of air then exhaled loudly, repeating the process several times. He wiped his eyes dry with the back of his hands. "I've already talked to Epps. His team has already taken over. It should have been Avril, but apparently she hasn't shown up, so he was called in."

Morrison frowned and it was Leroux's turn to notice something was wrong, and his jaw dropped as the conversation he had heard but not listened to finally registered.

"Has something happened to Avril?"

18

Morrison sat in one of the guest chairs. "Echo Team just found her body."

Leroux inhaled sharply.

"It looks like she committed suicide. The note she left suggests she did something she regrets, perhaps Agency related."

Leroux recoiled at the idea. "Not her. She loved her job. She loved working here. There's no way she would betray the Agency."

"That's what I thought until five minutes ago. It's too early to say exactly what's going on, but we'll get to the bottom of it. For now, go to the hospital, do whatever you need to do. Just keep me posted."

"Yes, sir." Leroux rose and headed out the door as Morrison returned to his chair behind his desk. It was a bad day for the Agency, and he just prayed things didn't get worse, for if Casey were indeed a traitor, she was privy to so much information, covers could be blown the world over, including his best friend's.

Dylan Kane.

Beijing Capital International Airport

Beijing, China

CIA Operations Officer Dylan Kane stepped up to the Chinese customs official with a smile. He had been to China countless times, and when he came through the front door, it was always using his cover as an insurance investigator for Shaw's of London, and his cover demanded he play the part. His bespoke Savile Row suit cost more than three months of his regular paycheck, the tie alone a healthy car payment. And his CIA-customized watch, now sending an electrical pulse into his wrist in a pattern that indicated he had an urgent message from Langley, was TAG Heuer.

Unfortunately, the timing couldn't be worse.

He smiled at the man on the other side of the glass as he handed his passport and paperwork over.

"The purpose of your visit?"

"Business, then hopefully a little bit of pleasure."

The man scanned the passport and the visa. "You come here quite frequently."

"Yes, I do. China's part of my territory."

"And what do you do, Mr. Kane?"

"I'm an insurance investigator for Shaw's of London." He produced a business card. "One of our clients had his yacht stolen while he was visiting your country. I'm here to investigate."

"You don't trust that the Chinese police can do their job?"

Kane smiled, not taking the bait. "Oh, I investigate in a different way. Your police are concerned with the criminal aspect, I'm more concerned with the negligence aspect. You'd be amazed at some of the stupid things rich people do with their toys, then expect us to pay."

The man handed Kane's documentation back after stamping the passport with a flourish. "Enjoy your stay, Mr. Kane."

Kane smiled. "Thank you. You have yourself a good day." He casually headed toward the bathrooms and secured himself in a stall. He entered a coded sequence around the watch crystal and a message was projected on the glass that had him frowning.

Possible security breach at HQ. Cover may be compromised.

He acknowledged receipt of the message then flushed the toilet. He could abort the mission, though if his identity had been compromised, that still might not save him. Nothing drew attention more than stepping off an airplane then booking a last-minute flight to immediately leave. He had no choice but to continue to his hotel. Langley had indicated a possibility of his cover being blown, not a certainty. He needed more information, and the fact Langley had sent the urgent message, knowing the timing of everything, suggested they knew little about what was actually going on as well. That could all change by the time he arrived at the hotel.

He had a job to do, and unless he was given a direct order or agreed that his cover truly was blown, he intended to complete that mission. It was too critical to not go through with over possible suspicions. Besides, the Chinese likely already suspected who and what he was. The key was making sure he was never caught in the act. His country was well aware of who many of the Chinese spies were operating back home. The trick was identifying them and monitoring them. If you arrested them, then they would be replaced the next day with somebody you would then need to find, and they could operate freely for months or years before that happened. It was only when they were doing something overtly dangerous that you took them down, then used them as bargaining chips when one of your own was captured.

He emerged into the arrivals area and spotted his driver holding up a sign with his name. He was a low-level local asset that Kane had used before. The man didn't know who Kane actually was, but was paid to know the city like the back of his hand, to drive like a maniac if needed, and to not ask questions, yet have the answers about the seedy underbelly of Beijing the Chinese government would have the world believe didn't exist.

"It's a pleasure to see you again, Mr. Kane," said Xu Peng as he bowed deeply, taking Kane's bags.

"Good to see you too, Peng. It's been a long flight. Let's get to the hotel."

Xu led them outside and to a waiting SUV. Kane sat in the rear and as soon as they were off the airport grounds, he pulled out his phone and placed a secure call to Control. He was surprised when the familiar voice of his best friend, Chris Leroux, wasn't on the other end, and doubly surprised when it was Epps and not the scheduled backup Casey.

"This is Control Actual. Go ahead."

"It's me. I got your message. Does it have something to do with why I'm talking to you and not our friend?"

Even though he trusted Xu, it was only to a point. He had to be careful what was said. "Not your friend, but his backup. A lot's happened here in the past couple of hours. There is a chance that we've been compromised. We don't know the extent of the damage, if any."

"When will you know?"

"We may never know. There's a possibility the backup I was called in to replace had two employers, if you know what I mean."

Kane did, and the implications were staggering. If Casey, who had been at the Agency for years, was working for the other side, she had access to incredible amounts of classified intel. She would be privy to the identities of people like him, the assets they employed, safe houses, communications protocols, missions. It was endless. The question was, whose asset was she? Chinese, Russian, Iranian, North Korean? It was only a problem for him today if she were working with the Chinese. "I assume she's being questioned?"

"No, it appears she committed suicide last night because of what she's been doing."

A pit formed in Kane's stomach. Casey, dead by her own hand. None of this made any sense. He had met the woman and she always seemed so full of life, yet if she were a traitor, then he had obviously misjudged her.

And perhaps the happy person he thought he knew was merely a façade to disguise a tortured soul.

The situation with Casey was interesting, but it didn't explain why Leroux wasn't on the job, or at least one of his team. "What about my friend?"

"Something else happened. Sonya Tong was shot on a city bus this morning. Leroux is at the hospital."

"What? Is she all right?" Kane had worked with the woman for years, usually over an earpiece, but more recently in person. She was exceptional at her job and one of the nicest people he had ever met. For her to be shot was unfathomable. People like her were supposed to be constants in your life.

"We don't know yet. Last I heard is she's in surgery. The news is reporting her as clinging to life."

"What happened?"

"The same thing that happens every damn day in this country. Some nutbar with a gun aired his grievances, this time on a city bus. He shot the driver then several other passengers while screaming about people watching him and following him."

Kane's head slowly shook. His country was going to hell in a handbasket over a uniquely American problem. There wasn't a civilized country in the world that had this issue, yet as with most of America's problems, there was no civil discourse. One side wanted no restrictions, the other wanted total bans, and those in the middle weren't given the time of day by either extreme. It meant nothing would ever be done, and the carnage would continue thanks to the binary society where one side is absolutely right, and the other side is absolutely wrong.

No middle ground.

He sighed. "Keep me posted, and pass on my prayers if you get a chance. Now, back to the first problem. When do you think you'll know, if ever, how we've been compromised?"

"Unfortunately, I think it's 'if ever,' but it's way too early. It hasn't even been an hour. I've spoken to the Chief. Some ops have been scrubbed already, but yours is considered too important. He said it's up to you unless we get something concrete. We need that intel, and at the moment, you're the only way we can get it."

Kane had to agree. Their asset had demanded an in-person meeting. He didn't want it transmitted in any fashion. The intel was apparently explosive, something that could change the balance of power in China if used correctly. And that balance desperately needed to be tilted to the more reasonable side of things than the current leadership, hell-bent on world domination. "I agree with the Chief. You keep me posted if there's anything specific. Otherwise, I'm proceeding."

"Understood. Good luck."

"Thanks. Let's hope I won't need it." He ended the call and leaned forward. "You, of course, didn't hear any of that."

"Of course, sir."

Kane chuckled. "But keep an eye out for anybody following us. If we are compromised, you know your cover story. Just stick to it. They might try to break you, but as long as you stick to the story, you'll eventually be fine."

Xu checked the rearview mirror. "My girlfriend will be very upset if they mess with my face."

Kane laughed. "Let's hope they leave the money maker alone. In fact, let's hope we're worrying about nothing."

Inova Fairfax Hospital
Falls Church, Virginia

Leroux sat in the ICU waiting room, two fingers rapidly tapping on each armrest. It had been fifteen minutes since he arrived, and all he knew was that Tong was still in surgery. He had no idea if that was a good thing or bad, expected or unexpected. Was an hour in surgery normal for a routine gunshot? He would have to think anything as traumatic as a gunshot, even if it weren't life-threatening, needed an hour on the table, but right now he had no idea if a doctor would be coming through the doors in six seconds or six hours. He was certain longer had to be worse, though longer also meant she was still alive, and there was still a chance to save her. If those doors swung open now, he had no idea what the odds were, but he had to guess they were against her, and the sooner those doors opened, the sooner he could be finding out that his dear friend had lost her battle and was dead.

A doctor walked up to the nurses' station and the woman behind the desk pointed directly at Leroux. The man walked over and Leroux shot to his feet.

"Are you Sonya Tong's husband?"

He was surprised at how good that mistaken identity felt. "No. I'm her supervisor and friend."

The doctor looked about the room. "None of her family is here?"

"No. My team and I are her family here. HR is contacting her relatives, but I haven't received an update on when they can be expected. They don't live anywhere near here. Just tell me, is she still alive?"

The doctor's eyebrows rose slightly as if he were surprised at the question. "Of course she's alive. It was just a round to the shoulder. I managed to remove the bullet and repair the damage. She lost a good chunk of blood, but we gave her a transfusion and she's stable. She'll have a scar and she'll need some physio, but she'll make a full recovery."

Leroux's shoulders slumped with relief. "But on the news they said she was clinging to life?"

The doctor grunted. "Well, that'll teach you to listen to the news. They weren't referring to her. We have several patients in surgery right now from that incident. And one of them…" He paused. "One *was* clinging to life, but we weren't able to save her. She died on the table about fifteen minutes ago."

Leroux closed his eyes, saying a silent prayer for the lost soul, and also begging God for forgiveness that he was relieved it was a stranger that died rather than his friend. A thought occurred to him that had his heart racing. "Has that news been made public?"

"Not officially, though I have no doubt it's been leaked. Everybody wants their fifteen minutes."

Leroux cursed, grabbing his phone from his pocket. "If it's been leaked, then Langley knows and they're going to think she's dead. Can I see her?"

"In about an hour. They're just situating her now in recovery, and you've got to give her some time for the anesthesia to wear off. I'll let the nurse know that even though you're not family you're cleared to see her."

"Thank you, Doctor. It's appreciated."

The doctor bowed slightly then left the waiting area as Leroux dialed Morrison.

"Hi, Chris. I'm so sorry, I just heard."

Leroux ran his fingers through his hair, pulling hard, hoping the pain would stem the tears that threatened to flow. "No, sir, it wasn't her. She's not the one who died."

"What?"

"It was someone else. The news was right, but they were talking about someone else. Apparently, there are several people in surgery. I just spoke to the doctor. Sonya took a round to the shoulder but she's expected to make a full recovery. He said I can see her in about an hour. It was another woman that died."

"Oh, thank God." Morrison cursed. "You know what I mean."

"I know, sir. I had the same reaction."

"Okay, I'm going to hang up now. You call your team, because if I misinterpreted what I heard, you know they did."

"Yes, sir. Thank you, sir." Leroux ended the call then dialed the operations center as Lee Fang rushed through the door, tears flowing, and he had to think she had heard the news report, misinterpreting it like everyone.

She quickly rushed up to him. "I'm so sorry. I got here as soon as I could when I received your message. I just heard on the radio—"

He held up a finger as Therrien answered, the man's voice as somber as Leroux had ever heard it.

"Marc, this is Chris. She's not dead. It wasn't her."

"What?"

"It wasn't her. It was someone else that died. I just spoke to the doctor. Sonya's going to be all right. She's already out of surgery."

"Oh, thank God! Everybody, listen up! Sonya is alive! It wasn't her! It was someone else! Chris says she's out of surgery and will be all right!"

Cheers erupted in the background and Fang hugged him, her sorrow replaced with joy.

"You're not messing with me, are you?" asked Therrien.

Leroux smiled. "No. The doctor has cleared me to see her even though I'm not family. As soon as I do, I'll let you guys know what's going on. She took one to the shoulder and they said they removed the bullet and repaired all the damage and replaced the blood she lost. She's going to be fine. I'm going to let you go now. You just make sure that word spreads far and wide that she's alive. Oh, and call HR. The last thing we need is them updating her employment records to indicate she's dead. God knows when they'll get her paychecks flowing again."

Therrien laughed. "That's no joke. That happened to a friend of mine. I'll call them right now."

"You do that. I'll talk to you soon."

Leroux ended the call then embraced Fang with both arms as they sobbed with relief. He had few friends in this world, even fewer good friends. Lee Fang was Kane's girlfriend, and they lived together in the same building as he and his partner, Sherrie White. The four of them were very close, and with Kane and Sherrie out of the country on ops, he had messaged her about what was going on while he waited for word.

"You didn't need to come," he said.

She patted his chest as she broke the embrace. "Nonsense. I wasn't going to let you go through this alone. I know how important she is to you."

Leroux's stomach flipped as if he had been caught cheating on Sherrie. "She's a good friend."

"I know. And I know how she feels about you."

Leroux feigned ignorance. "What do you mean?"

Fang gave him a look. "Don't play dumb with me. A woman knows. And besides, Sherrie told me."

Leroux groaned, rolling his eyes. "For a spy, she's terrible at keeping secrets."

Fang grinned. "There are no secrets between best girlfriends."

"Uh-huh. Well, you know that I would never—"

"Of course not. I know you love Sherrie. It's not your fault that another woman loves you. And I know you'd never act on it. But it doesn't mean that you don't care, and it doesn't mean that you don't care more than you think you should. Don't feel guilty. Sherrie would understand." Leroux sat back down and Fang took the seat beside him. She gestured at his phone. "Now, is there anybody else you contacted who needs to know she's not the one the news is reporting as dead?"

"No, you know her. She doesn't have a lot of friends outside of work."

Fang leaned back and sighed. "It's so sad. She's such a sweet girl. She deserves to find someone that makes her happy."

Leroux put his head back against the wall and closed his eyes. He wished the same thing, and at this very moment, he wished he was that man.

Hotel Hilton Beijing Wangfujing

Beijing, China

Kane lay on the king-sized bed of the luxury suite at the Beijing Hilton. It was one of his favorites and he stayed here regularly when his cover was in Beijing. One thing the authorities liked was predictability. His cover always used the same airlines, the same hotels, the same drivers, and frequented the same restaurants.

But if he had been compromised, he had to vary things a little.

He had been shown his room and immediately rejected it when he looked out the window. A construction crane was within sight. For his purposes, it could have been anything. He would have picked a gaudy color if he had to.

"This view won't do."

This had caught his porter off-guard. "Sir?"

"Switch me to the other side of the hotel."

It had taken twenty minutes, but he'd been moved to another suite as requested. The view was worse. A frequent guest like himself, paying top dollar and tipping generously, was always given the best view on the first try, but he had feigned acceptance. If his host government had prepared anything special in his previous room, they wouldn't have had time to do anything substantial in his replacement suite.

He tipped the bellhop and closed the door. He pulled out his phone, launching an app that would search out any stray signals while he pretended to check his messages and nonchalantly toured the suite. His app reported three anomalous signals, one in the main area, one in the bedroom, and one in the bathroom. Routine fare, and nothing he ever worried about. This was the standard surveillance found in most high-end Chinese hotels so they could listen in on high-powered business executives. He never conducted business in his suite, but the fact it was only the regular surveillance gear detected suggested his switching rooms had successfully defeated any additional surveillance that might have been planned for him.

His watch indicated a message arriving through his private network. He rolled off the bed and walked to the window with his phone, wearing nothing but a smile. He leaned against the wall so the phone screen was opposite where the signal was detected, just in case it was video surveillance, which it likely was since it was the bedroom. The Chinese were always horny to get footage of a subject having sex—it could prove to be valuable blackmail material.

He logged into his private network and smiled at the message from the love of his life, Fang. Tong was going to be all right. She was with Leroux at the hospital now. Leroux had been his best friend in high school, a mismatch if there ever was one, and after drifting apart had been reunited when they discovered they both worked for the same agency, though in dramatically different capacities. Now, he couldn't imagine his life without him in it.

His friend had always been an introvert, painfully so, until Sherrie had drawn him out of his shell. The revelation that Tong had feelings for his friend had been almost comical. The poor guy hadn't known what to do with himself, and he had to be feeling horrible with what was going on. Sherrie White was an incredible woman. Beautiful, vibrant, talented, funny, the complete opposite of what he would have expected Leroux to end up with. Tong was more his friend's type, or at least that's what he had always assumed. Extremely intelligent though quiet, witty when she was comfortable, though still beautiful, but in a less obvious way than the head cheerleader type that Sherrie was.

His friend loved Sherrie and Sherrie loved him, and Kane was certain they could go the distance, but Sherrie was an operative just like he was. It was a dangerous life, and if something were to happen to her, he had always believed that Leroux and Tong would get together, though Kane might have to force the issue like he had before.

His watch pulsed with another message and he brought it up through the secure app on his phone rather than manipulate the highly classified device. Their asset had confirmed the meet. One hour. If the exchange was successful, he would take the intel to another contact who would transmit it securely, then he would leave the country as scheduled. If he was compromised, he just hoped he could get through the next two hours without being taken down.

And if he were, the intel that might cost him his life better have been damn well worth it.

Inova Fairfax Hospital
Falls Church, Virginia

Tong swam through the fog, desperate to find the source of the sound, a steady beep in the darkness. Her legs and arms slowly moved as she tread water, a thick mist obscuring the surface and anything beyond her hands. It was dark, but there was a light surrounding her, a gentle glow, and she had to assume it was the morning sun here to burn off the fog to let her see what was making the noise, to hear where it was coming from.

A gunshot rang out, then another and another. Her heart hammered and she reached forward to claw at the water in an effort to escape the danger, but she cried out at a horrendous pain in her shoulder. What was happening to her? Why was she in the water? Who was shooting at her? Why did her shoulder hurt? She needed help.

"Help me! Somebody, please help me!"

Someone took her hand and she gasped. "You're going to be all right."

She called to the voice, to the sound of someone with her in the darkness. "Where are you?"

He squeezed her hand a little tighter. "I'm right here, just open your eyes."

Her pounding heart settled slightly as she stared into the fog. "I don't understand."

"You're in the hospital. You just came out of surgery. The anesthesia is still wearing off."

She gasped. Her car that wouldn't start, her race to the bus stop, the handsome stranger, the lack of change, the tentative first date, the gunshots. She bolted upright, her eyes wide, reality clearing the fog. The beeping she'd been hearing was a machine to her left. She was in a hospital room, her shoulder ached, and she was as groggy as she had ever felt.

"Welcome back."

Her head spun toward the voice and she inhaled sharply. It was the handsome stranger holding her hand. He smiled that incredible smile.

"What happened?" she asked, still confused.

"You were shot on the bus. Do you remember?"

She closed her eyes, sniffing hard at the terrifying memory. She gave a curt nod. "I do." She opened her eyes and glanced at her shoulder, bandaged up. "Am I…"

"You're going to be fine, full recovery. It'll just take some time."

She lay back down on the bed, noticing he was still holding her hand and she was letting him. "Why are you here? Were you injured?"

"No, I'm fine. I just wanted to make sure you were all right." He held up his phone. "And I was hoping to get a name to go with this number."

A warmth spread through her body as the memories came flooding back of their brief encounter, the details vivid now. "Sonya."

He clasped her hand to his chest. "Sonya. Beautiful."

"Are you going to tell me your name?"

He chuckled. "Nathan. Nathan—"

"Hey, you're not supposed to be in here."

Nathan let go of her hand then rose, turning toward a nurse standing in the doorway. "I'm sorry, I just wanted to make sure she was all right."

"Well, now that you've seen that she is, I'll have to ask you to leave. Family only."

Nathan smiled at Tong. "It was a pleasure to meet you, Sonya. Can I come by tomorrow to see you?"

Tong's heart raced, the beeping betraying her feelings.

Nathan glanced at the monitor. "I'll take that as a yes."

She smiled and nodded.

He patted her good shoulder. "I'll see you soon."

The nurse gasped as he walked toward her. "Oh, my God, you're the one from the news! You're the one who killed the gunman."

Nathan didn't confirm or deny what the woman said, instead simply bowing slightly. "Have a good day, ma'am."

The nurse stared after him, her mouth agape, her head slowly shaking. "All those looks and a hero too." She stepped toward the bed, checking the monitors. "You're a lucky woman to have a man like that in your life."

Tong stared at the door. "We just met."

"Well, sweetie, a man like that doesn't come and check on a stranger out of the goodness of his heart. He's interested. The question is, are you?"

Tong wasn't about to answer an impertinent question from a nurse likely only interested in the gossip her reply could provide. Yet the smile breaking out at the corners of her mouth betrayed her feelings.

"I see that you are. I hope it works out for you, sweetie. How you met will be one hell of a story to tell the grandkids."

"Grandkids?"

Tong flinched at Leroux's voice at the door, and a wave of guilt swept through her as if she'd been caught cheating on her boyfriend. This was all so confusing and unfamiliar.

Yet it could be wonderful.

The Forbidden Palace

Beijing, China

Kane rubbed one of the ceremonial golden doorknobs on the massive doors to the Forbidden Palace. He needed all the luck he could get, and while he didn't believe in Chinese superstitions, they certainly couldn't hurt him right now. He strolled through the gates, playing tourist, leaving Xu waiting in the SUV. No tails had been spotted, though that meant nothing. This was his enemy's home turf. They could follow him by drone, satellite, CCTV camera, or have fifty agents assigned to him, none following him for more than two minutes. He had to assume they were watching him.

He spotted the asset standing near the Arrow Pavilion, the man fidgeting, shifting from one foot to the other, far too nervous to not be conspicuous. Kane strolled toward him, his phone in his hand, snapping several photos. He held out the device.

"Excuse me, sir. Do you speak English?"

His asset, Duan Guofeng, flinched, clearly uncertain as to what was going on. "Yes."

"Can you take my photo, please? I just hate selfies. I prefer things to look more natural."

Duan took the phone and Kane spoke without moving his lips, a long-practiced technique that could get him a well-paying gig on the Vegas Strip. "We're probably being watched. After you give me back my phone, I'll shake your hand. Palm me the intel." He stepped back, positioning himself so the palace was in the background, returning to normal speech. "Just tap the red button."

Duan did as told, saying nothing, fear in his eyes as his head whipped from side to side, paying little attention to the task at hand.

Kane smiled. "Thank you so much." He rejoined Duan, who reached into his pocket as he handed the phone back. Kane checked out the picture, horribly framed, then extended a hand. "Thanks again."

Duan shook it and something was pressed into Kane's palm. He wrapped his fingers around it as he let go. "You have yourself a good evening now." He froze his lips again. "Don't do anything until you hear from me." He flashed a smile then walked away, not looking back. He completed his circuit of the square, snapping another dozen photos before sauntering back to his waiting SUV.

Xu held open the rear door and Kane climbed in, Xu sealing him inside the sanctuary Kane was confident wasn't bugged, the tinted windows protecting him from any external surveillance. He opened his hand, squeezed shut since the exchange, a small USB key revealed. He had no doubt Duan wanted to explain what was on it, why it was so important, but if any of what he would have said was true, it was far too dangerous to have let him explain.

"Where to, sir?" asked Xu as he climbed in the driver's seat.

"Zhongguancun e-Plaza. I feel like being around people."

"Yes, sir." Xu put the vehicle in gear and they slowly pulled away.

Kane slipped the intel into his shirt pocket then leaned back, closing his eyes. In less than thirty minutes his mission would be complete, and he had to think that if he made it to his next contact, he was getting away with it, for surely the Chinese would have had enough time to review any footage taken of the exchange and confirm for themselves what had happened. The fact he and Duan hadn't been taken down the moment they shook hands had been a shocker. Epps had said they weren't sure what was going on, and from the moment he had heard of what they suspected Casey had done, he had had his doubts.

He was a good judge of character and simply couldn't see the woman betraying her country, at least not willingly or knowingly. Perhaps Langley was wrong about this. Perhaps she had merely committed suicide and they were misinterpreting her note. He sighed. He couldn't remember the last time he had wanted a mission to end so desperately. His family was hurting and he should be with them.

This intel better be worth it.

Outside the Forbidden Palace
Beijing, China

Duan Guofeng sat in his car, his entire body trembling as he gripped the steering wheel, his knuckles white, his palms sweating. Things hadn't gone as planned, not by a long shot. He was supposed to talk to Kane, to warn him, and to tell him he wanted out. His job at the Ministry of State Security provided him with access to a lot of intel, the trusted position earned with more than two decades of service. But years ago, his father had been killed in Tiananmen, and he had sworn if he ever had a chance to do something to exact revenge on his government, he would.

Street protests were ineffective with the Communist regime. You had to find something that embarrassed the leadership, to catch them doing something the public would find so appalling that the grassroot support would crumble, leading to the fall of those responsible.

And he had found it.

When he had come across the raw transcript of a debriefing that was never supposed to happen, a debriefing cut short when a senior Party official entered the room, he had been shocked. The recording should have been destroyed immediately, the transcript should have never been made, but somebody had screwed up.

Or, perhaps they hadn't.

Perhaps they wanted what had been said to be preserved, to somehow get out into the world where the shocking revelations might do some good. Whatever the reason, whatever the cause, it didn't matter. It had come across his desk, and the moment he saw it, he knew after all these years, he finally had something that could truly damage those in power.

His immediate instinct was to copy the transcript, but all network activity was monitored. He had instead taken photos of his screen, quickly flipping through all the pages, then moving on to the next file, though not before flagging the transcript as "Low priority. Enemy propaganda." If the records were reviewed, no one would ever believe he hadn't read the file and not reacted to it. When he had returned home that day, he had transferred the photos, making several copies before encoding a message and posting it on a dark web messaging board monitored by the Americans. His government was fully aware of the site, and one of his jobs was to monitor it, something he'd been doing for years.

Two years ago, he had made his first posting, warning the Americans that the site was compromised. To his dismay, his warning appeared to have no effect. A week later, he had found a file sitting on the desktop of his computer at home. How it got there, he had no idea, and his initial thoughts were to simply delete it. But the fact it said "Open me" in English had him double-clicking. It contained a web address and a password. It was a travel website featuring tours of the Great Wall. It appeared entirely legitimate. In the upper right corner, there was a small link, "Agent Login." He had clicked on it and entered the password, and his world had changed forever.

Within a week, he had met with someone Chinese who had vetted him, and after a few months, he had met with Dylan Kane, a man who seemed far too young for the responsibilities forced upon him by his country. What was strange was Kane had never asked him to do anything, and was never disappointed that there was nothing to report.

He had asked Kane about it, and the young man had simply shrugged. "One day, you'll come across something that we need to know, and you'll know that you can trust me. And when that day comes, I'll know to trust you because you've never wasted my time, so if you do come across something important, I'll know to believe you."

It made sense at the time, and it was proven three days ago when he had made contact outside of the normal schedule.

He released his grip on the steering wheel. He had done his job. He had delivered the intel. And if he was right, the Americans could use it to bring down the current leadership and, perhaps, a more moderate one would follow. He had no delusions about Chinese democracy. Perhaps someday, and he would be honored if he were a footnote in the history that would be written about it, but right now, he just wanted to get home to his wife and the weekly family dinner with his two adult children and their families that always brought him so much joy it stiffened his resolve to change his country for the better.

Somebody rapped on his window and he recoiled in fright. He couldn't see who it was, but he could see their finger pointing down, indicating for him to lower his window. He could start the car with the push of a button, put it in gear, and speed away, but where would he go? This was China. They would find him in a matter of hours if not minutes. His shoulders slumped and he pressed the button, the window slowly dropping out of the way. The man bent over so Duan could see his face. He was young, in a cheap suit, with an ID hanging around his neck, flipped the wrong way.

"I'm going to have to ask you to move, sir. We're closing this area for maintenance."

Duan nearly soiled himself in relief and his head bobbed furiously. "Yes, yes, of course. I'm sorry, I'll leave immediately." He started the engine and pulled away as the young man stepped back. He glanced in his rearview mirror to see him talking to his wrist, and his heart nearly stopped as the man turned his back on him. Had he imagined it? Was he merely talking to himself while he scratched his nose? Or was he indeed talking into a communications device, reporting back to his superiors about his encounter with the traitor?

What am I supposed to do?

Inova Fairfax Hospital

Falls Church, Virginia

"You can't be in here."

Leroux jerked a thumb over his shoulder at the nurse's statement. "The doctor said it was okay since she didn't have any family nearby."

"It's all right. He's my boss," said Tong.

"And your friend, I hope."

Tong smiled and the nurse rolled her eyes. "Sweetie, you've got them coming out of the woodwork. I wish I had whatever it is you have." She headed for the door and Leroux stepped aside. "Honey, the competition is stiff. Good luck."

Leroux gave Tong a puzzled look as he approached the bed. "What was that all about?"

Tong shrugged and winced, gripping her bandaged shoulder. "I'm not sure."

"How are you feeling?"

"Like I've been shot."

Leroux laughed. "That tends to happen when you get shot. I don't know what they've told you, but the doctor said they removed the bullet, repaired all the damage, gave you a transfusion to replace the lost blood, and says you'll make a full recovery, though you'll probably need some physio."

"What happened?" she asked.

Leroux patted the side of the bed and she nodded. He perched on the edge. "You don't remember?"

"Yes, I remember what happened. I mean, after I was shot I passed out, so I don't really know what happened after that."

"Oh, well, apparently the gunman shot half a dozen more people before one of the passengers grabbed him, managed to wrestle the gun away from him, then shot him. The details are still sketchy. I'm only going by what I've heard on the news. I haven't read any official reports yet."

"How many died?"

"Four, I think. For a few minutes, I thought you were one of them. We all did." His voice cracked and his eyes burned as he squeezed them shut. "I thought I'd lost you," he whispered.

She took his hand and he clasped it, opening his eyes to find tears rolling down her cheeks.

"I couldn't imagine my life without you in it."

She reached up and touched his face, wiping away a tear of his own that had escaped, sharing a forbidden moment, neither saying anything. He sniffed hard then let go of her hand.

"Why does life have to be so complicated?"

She wiped away her own tears. "It wouldn't be life if it weren't."

He grunted. "True enough." He inhaled deeply, squaring his shoulders as he forced the brave face. "The team sends their well wishes. You'll be happy to know that Randy was almost in tears, so when you get back you'll be able to tease him about that."

She giggled. "And here I thought deep down he thought I was a Chinese spy."

Leroux laughed at the memory. "Yeah, he definitely put his foot in his mouth that day."

"Speaking of the team, what's going on with the op?"

"I'm not sure. I handed control over to the backup crew."

"So, Avril is handling things?"

Leroux frowned at the mention of the woman's name.

"What is it? What's wrong?"

He sighed. "I wasn't going to tell you this since you've got enough on your mind, but Avril is dead."

Tong gasped, her heart rate monitor adding twenty beats. "What happened? How?"

"She didn't report in for her shift, so they sent someone to check on her. They couldn't get in, so Echo Team was sent. She committed suicide and left a note suggesting she might have been a traitor." Tong's heart rate continued to pick up and he took her hand. "Breathe. Just calm down."

Tong drew a deep breath then exhaled loudly repeating the process several times, her heart rate rapidly returning to normal.

"Okay, good. Last thing we need is you surviving a crazed killer just to have me kill you with words."

She laughed then frowned. "If it weren't you, I would say everything you just told me was bullshit. I've known Avril for years. There's no way she's a traitor. But more importantly, there's no way she committed suicide. We went out for drinks after work just two weeks ago. She was as happy as I've ever seen her."

"Depressed people can be experts at hiding their pain. Trust me, I know."

"True, but she was seeing a guy and it was becoming serious. She was in love, thinking of the future."

"You mean marriage?"

"Yes. I don't think they had talked about it yet, but she said it was a possibility. She said she could see them getting married and starting a family."

Leroux leaned back, folding his arms. "Huh. Maybe they broke up. Maybe that's what caused her to give up hope."

"It could be, but people break up all the time and they don't kill themselves. Something more had to be going on for her to do that." She pursed her lips, shaking her head. "It just doesn't make sense. I can't see her doing it. Yet, if she left a note..." She shrugged. "I don't know. Who would have thought a crazy day could get even crazier?"

"Yeah, it's been a little nuts, but don't you worry about it. You just focus on getting better. And I don't want to see you back at work until you feel up to it."

She gingerly rotated her left shoulder, grimacing. "It doesn't feel too bad."

He chuckled. "You just wait until the drugs wear off."

She groaned. "That's right, I forgot about that. I'll be back as soon as I can. With everything that's going on, you're going to need me."

"Everything that's going on?"

She gave him a look. "You know damn well that Sierra Protocol was initiated the moment they read that note. The entire Agency is going ape shit right now and the only reason you're not neck deep in it is because you're here with me."

"Exactly where I should be. But you can take it easy, the Chief hasn't enacted Sierra Protocol yet."

She gave his hand a quick squeeze. "Good, then maybe things aren't that serious." She yawned. "I'm exhausted and I'm about to fall asleep on you. So, why don't you go back to work? Thank everyone for the well wishes then come see me tomorrow."

He smiled as he rose, taking her hand once more. "If I can, I'll come by this evening and give you an update."

"Thanks, boss."

He eyed her. "I think you can call me Chris, don't you?"

She smiled. "Only out of the office."

He desperately wanted to give her a kiss, just a peck on the cheek, but lines had already been crossed. Instead, he clasped her hand in both of his then touched the entangled fingers to his chin. "I'll see you soon." He left the room, nauseated, guilt overwhelming him. He had always known deep down he had feelings for her, but this was beyond that. This was love, though there were various forms of love. Was this love for a woman that he wanted to be with, or was this love for a friend? And was the intensification of the feelings merely because of the situation? A traumatic event had happened. They had both given in to a moment of relief. Was he merely reciprocating her feelings for him out of sympathy?

He sighed. He loved Sherrie with all his heart and he couldn't imagine being with anyone else. And this situation with Tong and her feelings for him was something he had thought they had put behind them. When he found out, he should have insisted she be transferred, but that wouldn't have been fair. She had vowed she would be fine, and until now she had been. And in her defense, she had done nothing wrong today. He had been the one that had cracked, and she shouldn't be blamed for his weakness.

"What's wrong?"

He flinched, not noticing Fang approaching him. "Nothing." He needed to confide in someone, but she wasn't the one. She was best friends with Sherrie, and the last person in the world he wanted to hurt was the woman he loved. The only person he could think of to talk to was Kane, but he was in China on a critical op where if Casey indeed were a traitor, he might be in extreme danger. He gently shook his head. "It's just difficult to see a friend like that."

"It is, especially someone you care about." She took his hand. "Don't feel guilty. You're only human."

He gave her a weak smile. His raw emotions had exposed him, and his shoulders slumped. "If I shouldn't feel guilty, then why do I feel horrible, like I'm betraying Sherrie?"

Fang led him to a row of chairs and they sat. She continued to hold his hand. "First, don't worry. I'm not going to say anything to Sherrie, because you've done nothing wrong. Second, and please don't take this the wrong way, but Dylan told me Sherrie's your first girlfriend."

Leroux flushed at the embarrassing statement. A man his age should have had far more than one girlfriend in his life, though if he were to have only one, he couldn't imagine better. He was the envy of every man who had ever met her.

"Sonya cares for you more than she should and you're not supposed to know that, but you do. She understands that she can never have you, and that's her burden, not yours. Because you're a nice guy and an empathetic person, you share her pain and take it on as your own. And that's fine, that's the type of person you are. You just need to recognize that what you're feeling is empathy for the situation. Once the situation is over, that empathy will end as well, and you'll both go back to the way things were. It's nothing to feel guilty about." She cocked an eyebrow, giving him a look. "As long as you didn't make mad love to her in there, did you?"

He laughed nervously. "Of course not, but…"

"But what?"

"We held hands."

Fang grinned, holding up his hand that she had been gripping the entire time. "Just like I am, comforting a friend?" She leaned in closer. "Do you think I want to jump your bones?"

He chuckled. "No, I suppose not."

"You suppose?"

He laughed. "Fine, you're right, I'm reading too much into things." He sighed, patting her hand then letting go. "Thanks, I needed that. You're right, it's just the situation and our history. I'll be fine."

Fang rose. "Good. I assume you're heading back to the office?"

"Yes."

"All right. I'm going to head home. Anything you want me to tell Sherrie when I speak to her?"

His jaw dropped as his chest tightened, his stomach suddenly in knots.

She roared with laughter. "You should see your face. It's priceless." She patted his cheek. "Don't worry, sweetie. That conversation's in the vault. Now, you get back to work and make sure my Dylan gets home safe, otherwise all bets are off."

Zhongguancun e-Plaza

Beijing, China

Kane strode through Zhongguancun e-Plaza, one of his favorite places in Beijing. The throngs of humanity browsing the hundreds of vendors, the top-of-the-lungs negotiations taking place all around him. It was thrilling. Locals and tourists alike intermingled, all levels of society, some there for the show, some there just to feed their families.

He slid a chunk of meat off a skewer, savoring every chew. He had no idea what it was, and though he spoke and read Chinese fluently, he made it a point to never question what was on offer. He merely pointed then paid. Whether he was eating pork or panda was irrelevant, it simply tasted delicious, though the thought it might be panda turned his stomach slightly.

Any creature that cute when it sneezed should never be on a menu, endangered or not.

He casually sauntered through the market, enjoying the view, his penchant for Asian women indulged tonight, though none of them compared to his Fang. She was everything he had always dreamed of, gorgeous, intelligent, athletic, outgoing. But most importantly, an empathetic soul who knew who and what he was, someone he could talk to, someone he could share anything with and who wasn't just a sympathetic ear, but an understanding one. She had been in the business. She knew the sacrifices. And she was well aware of what questions she could and couldn't ask.

She was everything he needed in his life.

And though his eyeballs were enjoying the sights, all those sights did was fire him up for when he returned home, because the best sex with a stranger could never compete with making love while staring into the eyes of the person you intended to spend the rest of your life with.

He drew the last morsel of meat off the skewer then tossed it into a nearby garbage bin. He took a seat on a bench, bowing his head and smiling at an elderly lady sitting on the other end. She returned the gesture then he leaned back, enjoying the view as his eyes roamed the crowd searching for anyone suspicious.

Unfortunately, there was still no evidence he was being followed. If he could spot somebody acting suspicious, it would set his mind at ease, for then he'd know where he stood. He would abort and head back to the hotel, tossing the intel if he had to. But the fact he hadn't spotted anyone told him nothing. It could be that the Chinese had extremely competent people assigned to him, or that they were merely hanging back, letting electronic eyes follow him. For now, he'd assume the latter, but take the risk regardless. Casey might have compromised him or she might not have, but he couldn't continue the mission assuming the worst. He simply had to plan for it in case it did come true.

He rose, giving the old lady another nod and smile, then headed outside toward Li's Photo, run by one of his contacts that had worked for the Agency for decades, and with Kane since the beginning of his assignment to this region. Chan Chao and his wife Bing were committed to the cause of a free China, and he just prayed he wasn't compromised, for if the elderly couple were arrested because of him, they would be shown no mercy, and their final days on this earth would be brutal.

And it would also mean he had failed to keep a promise, a promise he made to them, to get them out of China should things go wrong.

He spotted the shop ahead, the familiar safe haven making him warm inside. Hopefully, he wasn't about to bring doom down upon his friends, for that's what they were despite only ever seeing them in the line of duty. Chan had risked his life for Kane on numerous occasions, going above and beyond what he had been hired to do, and Kane owed him his life several times over.

Chan's shop was an exchange point where information could be passed back and forth, operatives could be resupplied. Chan had his own network of contacts established over the years that provided intel that would then be fed back to Langley or to operatives, like himself, in the field.

He made a show of patting down his pockets then pulled open the door to the shop he had been in countless times. A familiar chime sounded and Chan's impossibly short wife, Bing, glanced at him from behind the counter. "I'll be with you in a moment," she said in Chinese.

Kane gave no indication he understood the words, though flashed a smile and pointed at the floor where he stood waiting. The customer she was tending to left, and the moment the door closed, Bing switched to English.

"You shouldn't be here."

Kane's eyes narrowed. "Why, have you heard something?"

"Sierra Protocol. We're supposed to lock everything down until we hear otherwise. Do you know what's going on?"

Kane shook his head. He had received the automatic communiqué through his watch only minutes ago but he wasn't about to abort an op and go to ground only seconds away from completing it. He had no details to share beyond what Epps had told him earlier, but the woman wouldn't be cleared to know, not to mention any information he gave her could be revealed under torture and would confirm to her interrogators she was on the inside. What was more concerning was the fact Sierra Protocol had been enacted. It meant the Chief had decided the Casey situation was now critical, and it could mean he had been compromised. "I'm sure they have their reasons. Where's your husband?"

"As soon as Sierra Protocol was enacted, he packed up all our gear and took it to a storage facility we have, just in case."

Kane looked about, well aware that anything incriminating was kept in the back. "Did he get everything out?"

"I think so."

"Well, let's hope so." The door chimed behind him. He didn't bother looking as he pulled out his phone. "I've got some photos I took here of the Forbidden Palace. I know it's kind of old school, but can you print some photos for me? I always like to send an envelope of pictures of where I've been to my parents. They always get a kick out of it, but they don't like technology." He could see concern in her eyes.

"No problem. Which ones?"

He brought up his photo list, selecting all those he had just taken in the square. "These ones."

She pushed a card across the counter. "Email them to this address." She leaned to the side, looking past him. "I'll be with you in a moment, officer." It was said in Chinese.

Kane wagged the phone. "Sent. When can you have them ready?"

"Come back in one hour."

"Will do." Kane turned to find a uniformed officer standing in the doorway. Kane smiled pleasantly at him. "Excuse me." But the man didn't move. Kane's eyes darted to the window, spotting half a dozen more outside. "Can I get by please?" he asked, making to step around the man. A hand was extended.

"Please remain where you are, sir." The English was perfect, not a hint of an accent.

"What's going on here?" demanded Bing in Chinese.

Kane stepped back, raising his hands slightly as his worst fears were confirmed. The Agency had been compromised. The question was, were they here for him or for the Chans? Had he led the authorities to them, or was the timing merely coincidental? Yet none of that mattered at the moment. Whomever they were here for, he was about to be taken into custody and they would find the memory stick with Duan's intel.

He slowly stepped back from the officer. "Listen, I don't know what's going on here, but I'm just here to get some photos developed." The man said nothing and Kane continued to slowly back away toward the counter where Bing stood.

"You should stop harassing hard-working shopkeepers!" she continued in the same shrill voice Kane had heard her use on her husband countless times over the years, though it was almost always in jest or concern, rarely genuine anger. The two of them loved each other more than any couple he knew. She stepped off the stool she had been standing on, revealing just how short she was, then rounded the counter carrying a cricket bat and shaking it at her unwanted guest. "Does your mother know what you do, that you harass little old ladies?"

The man's eyes bulged and Kane felt a twinge of sympathy for the young man as he continued to back away from the confrontation, maintaining his character of the innocent customer while Bing continued hers as the disgruntled shopkeeper.

The officer noticed him getting too close to the door leading to the back of the shop, and pointed a finger at him. "You! Get back here!"

The cricket bat swung, smacking the arm down. He yelped in shock, not accustomed to resistance from the public. Bing swung again. "You get out of here! I'm a good citizen! I pay my taxes! I file my paperwork!" She swung again as the young man blocked the blow, retreating a step each time rather than taking down his attacker who was a foot and a half shorter and approaching fifty years his senior. She swatted him again, continuing to press her advantage, but expertly putting herself between the guard and the door, forcing the man's back toward Kane.

Kane gently swept aside the beads filling the doorway to the back as Bing picked up the pace of her attack, her screams covering any noise the thousands of pieces of round plastic might have made clanging together. He headed through the rear storage area where many briefings and resupplies had occurred, then into their bedroom.

"That's enough!" shouted the officer and Bing cried out.

"How dare you!"

Kane desperately wanted to help the woman, but she was doing this for him. He moved aside a rug in front of the bed then yanked open a trapdoor disguised in the floorboards. He stepped into the crawlspace then lowered the door, reaching out to reposition the rug as he hid his method of escape. The escalating confrontation was instantly muffled as the door shut, leaving him in inky blackness. He pulled out his phone and turned on the flashlight, guiding himself through the escape route Chan had shown him once his trust had been gained.

He wove his way on his hands and knees, passing through the crawl spaces of the row of shops. He didn't have much time. As soon as they discovered he had escaped, the entire area would be cordoned off. Right now, he had to put as much distance between him and the shop as he could, as quickly as he could, then find a place to hole up. Unfortunately, if the Agency had been compromised, none of his usual safe havens could be trusted.

But that was the next problem to deal with.

He reached the end of the escape route, positioning himself underneath another trapdoor. He turned off the flashlight then listened over his pulse pounding in his ears. He could hear a siren, but little else. He gingerly pushed up on the trapdoor, revealing a sliver of dim light, but nothing more. The siren increased in volume. He pushed the trapdoor aside, poking his head up. He was in a utility closet of a restaurant at the far end of the strip of buildings. He climbed out then closed the door. He ran his fingers through his hair, attempting to rid it of the cobwebs he had pushed through, then brushed off his dusty suit jacket and pant legs futilely. His suit was in desperate need of dry cleaning, and in good light, he would stick out like a sore thumb.

The doorknob rattled and Kane spun his back toward the door, wrapping his arms around himself, moving his hands up and down his back as he moaned. The door opened. "Hey, some privacy here!" he shouted angrily in Chinese.

"Sorry," replied whoever it was, the door slamming shut, the man buying Kane's ruse that a make-out session had been interrupted. He couldn't stay here long. He removed his jacket and tie then grabbed a baseball cap for the Beijing Shougang Ducks off a peg on the back of the door. He fit it in place, pulling the peak low, then opened the door. He peered down the corridor toward the exit, not bothering to look the other way. He didn't want his face seen unnecessarily, and those behind him weren't who he was concerned about. He closed the door then headed for the exit, pushing it aside and stepping out into the late evening, the sun long set. He broke to his left, away from Chan's shop, then tensed as an engine started behind him. The tires crackling on pavement grew closer, leaving him wishing he had his weapon.

"Get in the back! Get in the back!" came the harsh whisper of Chan behind him.

Kane spun to see the man leaning out the window of a beaten-up van. Kane didn't bother asking why he was there, he simply followed instructions, rushing to the back and opening the doors before climbing in and shutting them.

"Stay on the floor and don't say a word," said Chan from the front as they slowly accelerated, making a turn at the end of the alleyway. They drove in silence for several minutes with sirens wailing past them on too many occasions. "All right, I think we're out of immediate danger. I guess they were serious with this Sierra Protocol warning."

"I guess so," agreed Kane.

"My wife?"

"She was brilliant. She stayed in character. You would have loved it. She started beating the officer with a cricket bat, shouting at him about harassing little old ladies. I was able to escape thanks to her."

"That's my girl," murmured Chan, his voice cracking. Kane needed him in the game and not emotional—there would be plenty of time for that later.

"We need a place to hole up and regroup. If the Agency's been compromised, then none of my usual safe houses can be trusted."

"I have a place."

"Is it somewhere the Agency doesn't know about?"

"Yes. I've been planning for this day for a long time."

"Then let's get our asses there and figure out what we're doing next."

Chan sniffed hard. "I don't know about you, but I know what I'm doing next."

Kane knew exactly what the man meant. Chan was going to attempt to rescue his wife, and Kane was honor-bound to help, but first he had to get this intel to the Agency. He closed his eyes, cursing to himself. If the Agency was compromised, he couldn't send the intel—all communications would be rejected. There were only four people he could think of at the Agency that he could absolutely trust. The last he heard, Tong was undergoing surgery and Leroux would be holding vigil at her side. Sherrie was on an op in Russia, leaving only the Chief.

But how the hell could he get the intel to the Chief?

He needed more info. Was the Agency truly compromised, or had they merely been following him? If the Agency was compromised, what was the extent of it, and was the security breach over now that Casey was dead?

"Are you going to help me like you promised?"

Kane pursed his lips and inhaled through his nose. "You can count on me, my friend. But there's something we need to do first."

Director Morrison's Office, CIA Headquarters

Langley, Virginia

Leroux entered Morrison's office a little more calmly than earlier, though an emotional wreck despite Fang's assurances. He was racked with guilt, yet she was right. All these emotions were because of the situation. Once Tong was out of the hospital and back at her station, everything would be fine. He just wished Sherrie weren't out of the country. He wanted to hold her, to be held by her, to reassure himself that nothing had changed between them.

Morrison rose and rounded his desk, concern on his face. "How's she doing?"

Leroux shrugged. "Good, I guess."

"Did you speak with her?"

"I did. She'll be fine. She was just tired. She wanted me to thank everyone for their well wishes."

"What did the doctors say?"

"She'll make a full recovery, but she'll probably need some physio."

"Where was she hit?"

Leroux tapped his left shoulder. "The doctor said he got the bullet out and repaired all the damage. They gave her a transfusion. He didn't seem concerned. It was somebody else that was brought in that the news was talking about that was in critical condition. They didn't make it."

Morrison frowned, patting Leroux on the arm then guiding him into a chair. Morrison sat across from him, leaning forward, his elbows on his knees. "How are you doing with all this?"

"I'll be fine. Just a lot on my mind."

"You care for her, don't you?"

Leroux's eyebrows shot up, his heart racing. Was he that obvious? He looked away. "Well, of course I do. She's one of my team. She's a friend. I've known her for years."

"Son, I've seen the way she looks at you. That woman cares for you and you know it. And you care for her and there's nothing wrong with that. But I need to know, is your head in the game?"

Leroux drew a long breath, filling his chest, then exhaled loudly. "Yes, sir. I'll be fine. I'll have to talk to my team to make sure they're all good to go, but they're all professionals. I'm sure we can be ready in thirty minutes."

"Good, because everything's gone to shit since you left."

Leroux's eyes bulged at his boss' frank statement. "Sir?"

"After consulting with the Director, I enacted Sierra Protocol. Kane's op has been blown. We've lost track of him, and because of the protocol, we can't reach out, nor can he. He was last seen heading into Chan's shop to transmit the intel, but it never came through. The authorities hit the shop. Mrs. Chan was seen being escorted out, but Kane never came out. We don't know if they hit the shop because he went into it and they had been following him the entire time, or if they hit the shop and Kane just happened to be there."

"That'd be quite the coincidence."

"Agreed. Bottom line is one of my top operatives is missing and one of my analyst supervisors has killed herself, leaving a note suggesting she's betrayed the Agency. I need to know the extent of the damage, and who we can trust. Is the threat over now that she's dead, and how was she compromised? Was it willingly? Was she coerced? Did she plant something in our systems that's continuing to transmit data despite the fact she's dead? There are a million questions that need to be answered and as much as I hate to say it, I trust you and no one else."

Leroux shifted uncomfortably in his chair. "That's rather depressing, isn't it?"

Morrison grunted. "You should see how it feels from my end of things. Am I saying nobody can be trusted other than you? Absolutely not. But we've long suspected there's a mole in the Agency working for the Chinese. Have we found out who she was, or was she a patsy of the real mole? I want you to figure out a way to put my mind at ease."

"You can count on me, sir, but I'm going to need my people."

"How do you know you can trust them?"

"I can't, but I have an idea."

"What?"

"Give me my team. I'll split them in two, half in an ops center with me, half with Therrien. Each team will work the exact same set of intel and then I'll review their findings. If something conflicts or something's omitted, then we know there's a problem. But if everything's matching up, then either we're getting the answers we want because there is no mole in my team, or the mole can't risk hiding anything because then he'll be discovered."

Morrison rose, his head bobbing. "I knew you were the right person for the job. Now go get it done. I need to know who we can trust and I can't have this mole hunt going on for too long. With Sierra Protocol enabled, every asset and operative in the world is going to ground until they hear from us. The longer this goes on, the more this country can be compromised."

Leroux stood. "You can count on me, sir. I'll find your mole."

"Good. Just be careful. We have no idea how they'll react when cornered. Don't assume that just because you've known them for years that they won't slice your throat to protect their secret."

Leroux shivered at the thought it could be somebody he knew, still not comfortable with the idea it might be Casey. "I'll be careful, sir." He paused. "Any word on Sherrie?"

"No, and there won't be. All we know is she received the Sierra Protocol transmission, and if she obeyed the order, she's gone to ground."

"I understand."

Morrison placed a hand on Leroux's shoulder. "This is one of those cases where no news is good news, and right now we think the mole was working for the Chinese, not the Russians. Those two might be allies on paper, but they're certainly rivals in the intelligence world. Try not to worry. Just focus on the job, and the sooner you succeed, the sooner she's home."

Leroux gave him a weak smile. "Yes, sir." He headed out the door and down the corridor to the elevators, his heart heavy with the responsibility ahead of him.

Find the traitor in their midst.

And possibly bring a friend to justice.

Operations Center 4, CIA Headquarters
Langley, Virginia

Epps stood to the side as the ops center swarmed with security personnel. The compromised Chinese operation had been scrubbed the moment Sierra Protocol had been implemented. Her team had been escorted out one by one, all being taken for interrogation. Her actions had tainted everyone associated with her, and unfortunately, for the moment, everyone was guilty until proven innocent.

It wasn't the American way, but it was the Agency way. It was just too risky to assume someone was innocent when security had been compromised. For the moment, all they knew was that Casey had committed suicide and left a note suggesting she had betrayed the Agency, and still none of it was the woman he knew. Despite that, everything she had touched would be examined—equipment, work areas, operations, everything would be reviewed for anything out of the ordinary.

The man in charge of the team investigating, Neil Neary, turned to him, pointing at the workstation normally manned by Control Actual. "And this is her workstation?"

"It would have been today, yes. Just remember, she rotates just like we all do. This would have been her workstation last night, but the night before, it could have been any of the other ops centers."

"I understand that, but this is where she would have been working if she were here today?"

"Yes."

"Are there any personal belongings here of hers?"

"There shouldn't be. Nobody leaves anything personal here. They bring it in with them then out at the end of the shift. Everybody has their own office or individual workspace that they personalize, but in the ops center it's pretty much all business."

"Is there anything she would bring in normally with her?"

"I'm sure there was, but I didn't work with her. I was brought in as a last-minute replacement because she didn't report for duty. I, of course, know her from around the office and have coordinated with her on many occasions, but I've never worked an ops center with her."

"You've worked closely with her?"

"At times, yes."

"Then I'm going to need you to come with me for questioning."

Epps suppressed the urge to roll his eyes. "Of course, anything that gets us back up and running."

Leroux stepped through the doors and Epps quickly joined him.

"You can't be in here," said Neary.

Leroux ignored him. "I need to know everything you know. The Chief's assigned my team to get to the bottom of this."

Epps nodded. "Good. The sooner the better."

"I said you can't be in here," repeated Neary, annoyed.

Leroux glared at him. "Talk to the Chief."

Epps cleared his throat. "This is Mr. Neary. He's in charge of the investigation."

"And who are you?" asked Neary, stepping away from the Control workstation.

"Analyst Supervisor Chris Leroux. My team has been assigned to determine the extent of the damage and who else might be involved."

"That's my job."

"Talk to the Chief." Leroux twirled his finger at their surroundings. "I assume this room is being locked down for your investigation?"

"Yes."

"And you are aware that she's worked in every ops center we have?"

"Yes, I am."

"Well, I'm going to need two ops centers immediately."

"Out of the question. They're all being swept and all the equipment is being seized any place she's been."

"I don't care about that. We have protocols in place. I need the rooms and I need them reequipped and I need it done immediately. We've already got a compromised op with a missing operative and hundreds of operatives and thousands of assets around the world going to ground waiting for word from us. The intelligence capability of this country is on complete hold until we determine the extent of the damage and whether it's safe to resume operations."

"And I don't work that way." Neary stepped closer and Epps was impressed that Leroux didn't appear intimidated. The kid had come a long way in just a few short years. There was a time when he would have pissed his pants and run for the door, but not anymore. And despite Neary being twenty years Leroux's senior with forty pounds on him, the young man wasn't backing down. "It takes time to conduct a proper investigation and I won't have you compromising it."

Leroux stabbed a finger at the team tagging and bagging all the equipment. "When they're done, what's going to be left in this room besides the desks?"

"We won't know that until we do a proper sweep."

"How long does it take you to scan a room?"

"Properly? Hours."

"We don't have hours. Lives are at stake. I need two rooms. Strip it bare, do your scans, and then my people are moving in. Take it up with the Chief if you've got a problem with that. Epps, you're with me." Leroux spun on his heel and headed for the door. Epps followed, grinning.

"I need him for questioning."

"And you can have him when I'm done with him."

Epps followed Leroux into the hallway and headed down the corridor away from the flurry of activity. "Holy shit, Chris. Did your balls get a refit?"

Leroux growled. "My best friend is missing, my girlfriend has gone to ground because we don't know who she can trust, another friend is in the hospital shot, another's committed suicide, and I'm told to assume I can't trust anybody while I'm tasked to find out just what the hell's going on. Assholes like that on power trips slow things down and put lives at risk. He knows damn well that no mole is going to leave behind a piece of equipment inside an ops center. They're scanned between every op and if it were found, we'd know something was going on and the list of suspects would be pretty damn narrow. That guy has a checklist that he's been working on for years just for this moment, and every second item on it is 'eff with everyone I can.'"

Epps desperately wanted to cheer every word Leroux had just said, for it was exactly how he felt as well, but never would have had the balls to say. He smiled, patting the younger man on the arm. "I agree with every word you just said, but you've got to calm down. He's following protocols that have been agreed to by his supervisors."

"Those can be overridden."

"But you don't want to put the Chief in an awkward position because you get into a pissing contest with a walking clipboard."

Leroux inhaled deeply, delivering a curt nod. "You're right, of course. I just don't have time for bullshit."

"I agree. Why do you need two rooms?"

"I'm splitting my team in two. Everybody's going to work the same intel. That should force the mole either to pass on anything he finds because he doesn't want to risk a discrepancy being detected, or there is no mole and everything will match up. Either way, we'll be able to trust the results of our investigation."

"Good thinking. Let me know if you need a hand."

"Thanks, but I don't trust you, remember?"

Epps laughed then pointed at the phone gripped in Leroux's hand. "Call the Chief. Give him a heads-up on the shitstorm you just started. I have to go and get grilled about a woman I considered a friend and convince them I knew nothing about what she was doing without making them suspicious that I'm covering for her."

Leroux sighed. "And that's the problem, isn't it? None of us knew this was happening. Hell, I still can't believe it's happening. I didn't know her that well, but I worked with her for years. If she could be a traitor…" He shook his head. "Any of us could be."

Epps leaned in closer, waving his fingers in front of his throat. "Ixnay on things like that. Clipboard's liable to take that as an admission of guilt."

Leroux chuckled. "Yeah, I guess we all better be careful about what we say until this is cleared up." He wagged his phone. "I've got a call to make. Good luck with your interrogation." He walked away and Epps joined the line of staffers being taken by elevator for their grilling.

This is going to be a long day.

Inova Fairfax Hospital
Falls Church, Virginia

Tong lay in the hospital bed, bored stiff. She had faked being tired so Leroux would get back to work. It was critical they get to the bottom of whatever was going on, and she cursed her bad luck that she had been caught up in America's shame.

She closed her eyes, replaying the tender moment they had shared. She still loved him, though perhaps that was too strong a word. Could it be called love if the entire relationship was in her head? Some might call it a crush, but to her that sounded like something teenagers suffered. Her feelings would go unrequited as long as Sherrie was in the picture, and she saw no way that would change unless something tragic happened to the operative now stranded in Russia until Sierra Protocol was lifted.

She had always known he was sympathetic to her feelings for him, but that was just because he was a good guy, one of the reasons she was attracted to him. But today, he had shown genuine feelings that went beyond just concern for a colleague. He truly cared, and it confused her even more. Perhaps she should move on, make a clean break and request reassignment. At least then she'd only face him in the corridors or elevators for a brief moment.

She sighed.

Or you could move on emotionally.

She smiled as she thought of Nathan. He was clearly interested, and she was as well, though she'd have to get to know him before she could be certain there was any possible future there. She had been in his presence less than five minutes and knew nothing about him except his name. Though that wasn't necessarily true. He was well dressed in a business suit. That suggested he worked in an office and was reasonably successful. He was getting on a local bus, so he lived in her neighborhood, a solid middle-class area, that further suggested he was reasonably successful.

The fact he had a bus pass indicated he was a regular user. You didn't live in her area if you couldn't afford a car, so it could indicate he was either environmentally conscious or didn't want to waste money on parking and the additional insurance. Or he could be an alcoholic who got into a car accident and had his license suspended.

She snickered.

You're such a pessimist.

She would love to be back at the office and run his name from the police report, though she couldn't do that. It was illegal. Yet she could go to security and say she'd been approached by a man and needed to know if it was safe to start seeing him socially. The CIA was always concerned about their staff being taken in by foreign operatives, but she was certain that wasn't the case here. It was too random. In order for the meeting to be arranged, he would have had to know her car wouldn't start today, to be at the right bus stop at the right time, and then, of course, there was the madman.

No, Nathan was the real deal. An attractive man interested in her after only a brief meeting. Love at first sight? Perhaps for him, but definitely not for her. Unfortunately for poor Nathan, her heart was taken. If she gave the man a chance, she might finally move on and leave her feelings for Leroux behind, which would allow her to continue working with him in a job she loved.

There was a knock at the door and the nurse stepped in holding a bouquet of flowers in a glass vase. "Something just arrived for you."

Tong smiled. "They're beautiful."

"They are, aren't they?" The nurse placed the flowers on the windowsill then fished the card out, handing it to Tong.

"They must be from the office."

"I don't know about that. A dozen yellow roses with one red one in the center? That's from someone who'd like to be sending you a dozen red roses."

Tong flushed. She wanted to think they were from Leroux, but he would never think to do such a thing, even if he weren't in a committed relationship already. She opened the card.

It was so nice to meet you,

I'm sorry you got shot.

Is it too soon to tell you,

I like you a lot?

Nathan

She giggled.

The nurse smiled as she checked the monitors. "I told you that wasn't from the office."

Tong pressed the card against her chest. "How could you tell?"

"Because a woman doesn't smile like that about her coworkers."

Tong gestured at the monitors. "How's everything looking?"

"Good. I read your file and it looks like the surgery was a complete success. You'll be back to normal in no time. How do you feel?"

Tong shrugged then cringed. "If I stop doing that, perfectly fine."

"You're not weak?"

"No. Though I could be running on a little bit of adrenaline still. There's something going on at the office that I really should be there for."

"Well, I think they can do without you."

"You would think."

The woman chuckled as she headed for the door. "Oh, honey, I hear that." She left then Tong opened the card again, rereading the bad poetry from Nathan. He was bold, there was no doubt about it. It made her wonder if he was a player chasing down every woman he could, hoping to play the odds that someone would eventually say yes.

She cursed herself.

Was it so hard to believe that a man could actually be interested in her? What had she presented to him? A well-dressed, attractive professional who lived in a nice neighborhood, who had invited him to sit with her. It was brief encounters like that that led to many of the great romances in books and movies. Why couldn't it be in real life?

She sighed, leaning back and closing her eyes, holding the card against her chest.

Please let this be the beginning of something wonderful. I deserve to be happy.

Chan Safe House

Beijing, China

"It's safe."

Kane sat up as the driver's side door opened and Chan climbed out, the van shaking slightly. The rear doors opened and Kane slid out, slapping Chan on the arm. "Thanks for the save, buddy."

Chan grunted. "I wasn't there for you, I was there for my wife, but I figured you wouldn't use the escape route alone if there was any chance of saving her."

"You're right about that. Like I said, *she* saved *me*."

"And now it's time for us to save her." Chan led him through a door and into what was the second half of a converted garage, a small bachelor pad set up. There was a bed, a walled-off bathroom in the back corner, and a kitchenette with a sink, hot plate, and rice cooker. Along one wall were bins of supplies.

"Looks like you're well provisioned."

"We could stay in here for months without leaving, if we have to." Chan pointed at a large cabinet against the far wall. "Guns, body armor, comms, pretty much everything you can think of are in there. Leftovers from scrapped missions and operators that never showed. The CIA always instructed me to dispose of anything not used, but I don't believe in wasting perfectly good equipment."

"Okay, we could start a small war, but that's not really going to help us get your wife out. What do you want to do?"

Chan dropped into a chair, his shoulders slumping as he exhaled loudly. "I don't know. This is where you and your agency are supposed to be helping, but with this damn Sierra Protocol, we're on our own."

Kane sat beside the man in a chair likely normally occupied by Bing. "How much time do you think we have?"

"It depends on what's going on. You know I've always had the shop set up so that we could bail on a moment's notice. As soon as Sierra Protocol was announced, I moved everything into my van and brought it to a storage location. There are no cameras in the back alley so they shouldn't know to trace it. I picked up that thing"—he jerked a thumb toward the wall behind which the van that had brought them here was parked—"then came back to get her, but it was too late. Bottom line is, they should find no evidence in the shop of what we're involved in. She'll stick to the story that you were just a customer and plead ignorance as to where you went."

"What if they know who you are and what you are, which we have to assume they do," interjected Kane.

Chan frowned. "Yes, you're right, I guess we have to assume that, so they're not going to believe anything she says."

"Do you think they'll torture her?"

Chan squeezed his eyes shut, fighting tears. "With this leadership, absolutely. What I don't understand is why did they act now?"

Kane regarded his friend. The man deserved the truth. "What I'm about to tell you is highly classified, and I can't even confirm it's true. This morning, Langley local, one of our analyst supervisors, think Control Actual, was found dead. It looks like she committed suicide, and the note she left behind suggested she had betrayed the Agency. She's been involved in any number of ops. That triggered Sierra Protocol. Until the Agency can figure out the extent of the damage and how far it was compromised, we're on our own. If she was working for the Chinese, they could simply be taking advantage of what intel they do have before it becomes useless, rounding up any of our assets and operatives before everything was changed. Or"—Kane patted his pocket with the USB key—"this could have nothing to do with that, and instead have to do with this intel."

"Just what is this intel?" asked Chan as he rose and grabbed two bottles of water from a nearby fridge, handing one to Kane.

"I don't know. All I know is it's supposed to be huge. It's critical that I get this transmitted to Langley. If your government catches up to us before I get a chance to do that, all of this will have been for nothing."

Chan took a swig of his water, screwing the cap back in place. "Unfortunately, with Sierra Protocol initiated, they won't be accepting any transmission from me. They'll assume I'm compromised." He scratched the stubble on his chin. "You said you have to get it into Langley's hands, but that's not necessarily true, is it?"

Kane's eyes narrowed. "What do you mean?"

"Well, you just need to get it out of this country. Why don't we transmit it to that little operations center you have, then it's secure in the United States on one of your servers. Then just make sure someone you trust knows it's there, and then we don't have to worry about it anymore."

Kane smiled slightly at the idea. "You're right. I've been looking at this from the wrong direction. Do you have the equipment for us to transmit?"

"I've got everything you could imagine here."

Kane rose with a grin. "Then let's get to work so we can save your wife."

Kane/Lee Residence, Fairfax Towers

Falls Church, Virginia

Lee Fang stood in the shower, letting the water run over her ripped body as she rinsed off the sweat from an intense workout. She had always had a rigid routine that kept her in top physical condition, but when the man she loved was on a mission, she always picked up the pace a bit more in an attempt to distract herself. Add to that the fact Tong had been shot and the additional weight of seeing how Leroux had reacted to the news, she had thrown in an extra workout, giving her a chance to process things.

The words she had said to Leroux were true. It wasn't his fault for the way he felt, and it certainly wasn't his fault for the feelings Tong had for him. If Sherrie weren't her best friend, she wouldn't give it a second thought. She had made a promise to Leroux that she wouldn't say anything to his girlfriend, and she intended to keep her word. They were all friends, the four of them, and they all knew how they felt about each other. Leroux was devoted to Sherrie and would never dream of betraying her, but according to Kane, he was inexperienced when it came to love, and most men had no experience with being loved by two women at the same time. The poor guy shouldn't be punished for that, and Sherrie shouldn't be made to worry unnecessarily.

She grabbed her sponge and squeezed it several times under the water before shooting a generous dollop of body wash onto it. The secret was safe, and she had nothing to feel guilty about in keeping it from her friend. In a way, she was protecting Sherrie. She lathered up, closing her eyes and inhaling deeply, enjoying the pomegranate scent. She rinsed off and stepped out of the shower, glancing at her phone to see a message had come in over Kane's encrypted network. She dried her hands and brought up the app, reading what her boyfriend had sent. Her eyebrows shot up, and a smile spread.

Action.

Trinh/Granger Residence

St. Paul, Maryland

Tommy Granger groaned as his fiancé, Mai Trinh, smeared her naked body over his. What had begun as an innocent massage of his shoulder where he had been shot several weeks ago had soon turned into something more.

"How does that feel?"

"Like I was never shot."

She giggled. "Roll over."

"If you insist." He did as told and smiled as he stared up into the eyes of the woman he loved. She was incredible, and he couldn't believe how lucky he was to have found her. She was beautiful, intelligent, funny, sensual, sexual, the total package. And she was his best friend. In fact, she was the best friend he had ever had.

She leaned in and kissed him, and he lost himself in the moment.

His phone demanded his attention.

"Don't you dare!" gasped Mai as their oiled bodies intertwined.

"That could be God calling and I'd tell him to wait."

She cried out and so did he, the intensity incredible. She collapsed atop him, spent, as his entire body oozed into the memory foam.

"You're incredible."

She pushed up on her elbows and grinned at him. "You're not so bad yourself." She rolled off and he groaned. "I bet you're not thinking about your shoulder now, are you?"

He laughed, slowly rotating it, feeling no pain. "You give the best massages."

She hopped out of the bed, heading for the bathroom. "And you're the only man who'll ever know."

"Thank God for that." He grabbed his phone off the nightstand, his eyebrows shooting up at who had called—Lee Fang, Dylan Kane's girlfriend. There was no voicemail, but there was no way it was a misdial. Something was up, and the fact it was Fang calling suggested Kane was in trouble.

He redialed the number and Fang answered immediately. "Hi, Tommy, thanks for getting back to me."

"No problem. What's up?"

"I need your help. I can't explain it over the phone, but are you up for a few days' work?"

He smiled. "Absolutely."

"Then you know where to meet me. When can you be there?"

"Two hours?"

"Okay, I'll meet you there."

"See you then. Oh, can I bring Mai?"

There was a pause. "Does she know her way around a computer?"

"She can follow instructions, but no, she's not at my level."

"Well, I'm sure there are other things we can find for her to help with. If she wants to come, then fine. Just make it quick."

"Yes, ma'am." Tommy ended the call and headed for the bathroom where the shower was already running, doing the mental math of whether there was enough time for round two.

Duan Residence

Beijing, China

Duan parked his car then strode quickly toward the entrance of the apartment building his family called home. His entire body was shaking with what he had done, and Kane's warning they were probably being watched had occupied his thoughts entirely since it had been given. He had spent more time watching his rearview mirror than what was happening in front of him, but had spotted no one following him. Yet he was involved in intelligence, and he was well aware they could be following him by drone or satellite. Or they simply planted a tracker on his car. Anything was possible.

If they knew what the intel was that he was handing over, he had to think they would have taken him down by now. It was too important for them to risk letting it get into the hands of the Americans, yet the handover had happened. Had that been by design, or because they hadn't known? And why had Kane given the warning? What did the American know that he didn't? Something was going on, and what that was, he had no idea, but every minute that went by where he wasn't arrested suggested whatever had Kane concerned was on the American side of things and not the Chinese.

He stepped into the lobby and headed for the elevators, his head on a swivel. He had to get control of himself. He was acting suspiciously. The last thing he needed was a nosy neighbor aware of where he worked to make a call. He rode up the elevator in silence with several others, then stepped off on the ninth floor. He'd feel better when he was within the walls of his home.

His key hit the lock and his eyes narrowed when there was no flurry of activity on the other side of the door that usually accompanied the signal of his arrival. Something was wrong. His family should be home. His daughters and grandchildren were visiting. He was coming home much later than usual, but that should have only added to the excitement.

But there was nothing. Absolute silence.

Could they have left for some reason? He dismissed the thought. He pressed an ear to the door and heard nothing. The fact he could hear sounds from his neighbors through their closed doors, yet nothing through his own, suggested volumes. Either his family wasn't home, or there was something wrong. And the only thing he could think of that would keep his family silent was that the authorities were on the other side of the door waiting for him.

The question was, what to do?

There was nothing he could do to save his family by passing through that door. Once he was arrested, it was over for all of them. If he fled, everyone he loved would be arrested and thrown in prison, used as leverage to get him to surrender. Yet if he could reach Kane and tell him what happened, perhaps the Americans could get his family out.

It was their only hope.

He withdrew the key and placed a hand on the door.

Please forgive me.

The door jerked opened and he gasped at the man now facing him.

"Is there a reason you're not joining your family, Mr. Duan?"

Kane's Off-the-Books Operations Center

Outside Bethesda, Maryland

Tommy kept a wary eye on his surroundings as Fang entered the code on the hidden keypad of Kane's off-the-books operations center, two conjoined shipping containers buried in a storage yard in the middle of nowhere. The door hissed open and he breathed a little easier when they were inside and the door was secured behind him.

Fang had told them nothing on the drive here, though before they put on the requisite hoods after climbing in her car, he had seen the concern on her face. Something was definitely going on and it had to involve Kane. What he didn't understand was why Leroux or Tong weren't here. A thought had occurred to him when they had arrived and he had removed his hood. He had once asked why Kane had his own operations center if he were one of the good guys, and he had been told it was in case the shit hit the fan and the good guys could no longer be trusted.

Could there be something wrong at the CIA? The thought terrified him. If something was going on at the CIA, then getting involved could be extremely dangerous. He glanced over at Mai, her excitement at being here obvious. He shouldn't have brought her.

Fang headed for the main control room and Tommy followed. "Get us up and running as quickly as you can. I'm going to do a perimeter sweep."

"What can I do?" asked Mai.

Fang grabbed a clipboard from the wall and handed it to her. "Inventory. Make sure this list matches what we've actually got. It'll give you a good opportunity to familiarize yourself with where everything is."

Mai smiled. "I'm on it."

Both women left the room and Tommy went to work flipping switches and pressing buttons, and within minutes had the now familiar operations center ready for whatever might come. And the message that sat in the queue from a coded sender he recognized as Kane, addressed to another that he recognized as Fang, had to be what this was all about. He was tempted to open it, but he didn't dare. Fang was in charge and the message was addressed to her.

He brought up the security cameras on the rear wall then turned in his chair. He spotted Fang returning, and as she approached the door, he pressed the button to buzz her in. She waved at the camera. The door hissed down the hall, the containers slightly pressurized to keep any noxious substances on the outside.

"Are we up?" she called from down the corridor.

"Yes, ma'am."

"Good. Is there a message there for me?"

"Yes, there is."

"What does it say?"

Tommy hesitated. "I didn't look. I was afraid you'd shoot me."

Fang chuckled as she entered the room. "And you might just be right. Mai, join us. We're all in this together so we should all see this. We're a team now."

Mai hurried into the room, the clipboard clutched to her chest as Tommy brought up the message. They all leaned in and read it. It was from Kane.

"What's Sierra Protocol?" asked Mai.

Fang held up a finger, finishing the message. "It means the Agency believes it might have been compromised. They announce Sierra Protocol to all their operatives and assets. It shuts down all communications until the protocol is lifted. It means Dylan and Sherrie and everyone else are left to fend for themselves."

"What could have gone wrong?"

"There could have been a security breach of some sort."

"Would Leroux know?"

"Probably, but we can't risk reaching out to him right now because we could get him in trouble with what's going on." She wagged a finger at the message. "This is more important than what's going on at the Agency. Dylan's op has been compromised, one of his assets has been arrested, and he's now in hiding with her husband. But this piece of intel he referred to is critical."

"What intel?" asked Mai.

Fang gestured at the screen. "Bring up the attachment."

Tommy double-clicked on the file and a series of screenshots appeared, all in Chinese. Fang leaned closer, reading them, then her jaw dropped. "Unbelievable!"

Tommy eyed her, certain he had detected a hint of fear in her voice. "What is it?"

"Evidence that just might bring down the President of China."

Mai stepped back. "That sounds dangerous."

Fang glanced over her shoulder at Mai. "It is. If the Chinese find out we have this, we're all dead."

Chan's Safe House

Beijing, China

Kane lay on the bed, his eyes closed, though he was wide awake. Chan was pacing while they waited for news that Fang had received the classified intel. He had signaled an SOS that indicated for her to get the ops center up and running. She would have sought help, and that would likely be Tommy Granger. There was no one else she could bring in. This had to be kept outside the Agency. Leroux, Sherrie, Tong, and Child were aware of his secret setup. Tong was out of commission, Leroux and Child would be under scrutiny by the Agency, and Sherrie was in Russia. It would be up to Fang to save them, if saving were even possible.

His comms squawked in his ear, paired to the encrypted app on his phone, and he bolted upright, Chan spinning toward him.

"This is Arrow, do you copy?"

He smiled at Fang's voice, giving a thumbs-up to Chan. "I read you. Status?"

"Are we secure?"

"Yes."

"We've received your message."

"And the attachment?"

"Read."

"Assessment?"

"If it's legit, the implications are terrifying."

"What does it say?"

"You mean you haven't read it?"

"I couldn't risk it. We don't have the proper equipment here to securely open it. I just transmitted it."

"Do you want me to transmit it back to you?"

"Do it." His phone indicated a message received through the secure app. He brought it up and his chest tightened as he read through the screenshots. "Holy shit!"

"Yeah, that's what I was thinking too. Is this legitimate? Do you trust the source?"

"I trust that the source wouldn't try to bullshit me, so I'm sure *he* thinks it's real."

"What's going on at the Agency? Why Sierra Protocol?"

"One of the analyst supervisors committed suicide last night and left a note suggesting she had betrayed the Agency. Right now, they'll be trying to figure out the extent of the damage. My op has been compromised. Chan's shop has been taken down and his wife arrested. That can't be coincidence."

"There's another possibility," said Fang.

"What's that?"

"That the intel's fake and that they used it to expose your network. They suspected your contact was a traitor, gave him intel he couldn't resist getting to his handlers, then they just waited to see where he went."

Kane chewed his cheek. She was right. It was a classic taken straight out of the tradecraft playbook. Yet, again, the timing was just too coincidental. He paused. Casey killed herself, leaving the note knowing that it would be found. If he assumed she was working for the Chinese, did she kill herself because her taskmasters were about to act and take down people she knew? Or did they act because she killed herself and they were about to be exposed? It was the chicken and egg, but it was critical to know which. One meant he was exposed, one meant this was a well-planned takedown of a spy network, which meant the intel could indeed be fake, or this was a hastily planned op where his enemy was working with little information and they might not even know what Duan had handed over.

For now, he had no way of knowing what the truth was, and he would have to hope that Langley figured things out sooner rather than later. In the meantime, they had two jobs to do.

"What's the plan?" asked Fang.

"We need to get that intel into Chris' hands. Any idea how?"

There was a pause before she replied. "I have an idea. Leave it to me, I'll take care of it. Now, what do we do about you?"

"Forget about me. Our priority now is to rescue Bing. Tell Tommy to work his magic. Check the cameras around Chan's shop. Try to find out where they took her, then get back to me."

"We're on it. Be safe."

"You too. We don't know how bad things are at the Agency, so be careful."

OC Sub-level, CIA Headquarters

Langley, Virginia

Leroux stood in the corridor with his entire team, save Tong. Everyone was shaken up about what was going on, but the fact their coworker was no longer in any danger and could be back at work shortly had them more angry about what had happened to her than anything else. "All right, can I have everyone's attention?"

The side conversations ended.

"The Chief has put me in charge of trying to get to the bottom of what's going on. I've vouched for you all, however, we have to accept the possibility that one of us could be a traitor." Heads swiveled and he raised a hand, cutting off things before they got out of hand. "I'm not saying I believe anyone here is. I'm just saying we have to accept that there's a possibility, no matter how remote. I personally think it's bullshit, however, this situation means we can't be concerned with feelings. I proposed a plan to the Chief and he's agreed it's the best way to go about this.

"We're going to be splitting into two teams. I'll be leading Team One in OC-Two. Marc, you'll be leading Team Two in OC-Four. All intel that we discover will be shared between both teams and investigated thoroughly by both. Nothing will be split. The work will all be duplicated. That work will then be compared and any discrepancies flagged. That way, we'll get the answers we need. If there is a traitor among us, they're going to have to either expose themselves by creating a discrepancy, or potentially implicate themselves by passing on the correct intel that could lead to their discovery. Either way, we get our answers. Any questions?"

"What if we do have a traitor and we expose them?" asked Child.

Leroux jerked a thumb over his shoulder at members of Echo Team. "Two members of Echo Team will be in each room, fully armed. If the traitor does try to harm anyone, they will be taken down. I don't think you have anything to worry about. Let's just do our job, do it well, and find out what the hell is going on. We need to prove whether or not Avril was a traitor, and if she was, just how far was the Agency compromised. The sooner we have those answers, the sooner we can end Sierra Protocol and get our people home. Any more questions?"

Heads shook.

"Good." He indicated five of his team members. "You're with me, the rest with Marc. Let's get to work." The two teams filed into their respective operations centers as Morrison emerged from the elevators and flagged Leroux down.

"Are you ready to go?"

"Yes, sir, we are."

"I got an earful from Neary. You really pissed him off."

Leroux grunted. "He pissed me off."

Morrison regarded him. "A little piece of advice, son. Choose carefully whom you piss off. Guys whose job it is to investigate people like us independently, aren't the ones you want to make enemies of."

"He can crawl all the way up my ass if he wants, I've got nothing to hide. I just want to get to the truth as quickly as possible so we can get Sherrie and Dylan and everyone else back home safely."

"I understand. Just remember, that's his goal as well. He's just coming at it from a different angle."

"And what angle is that?"

"Everybody's guilty until proven innocent. He's good at his job. Let him do it. I'll try to keep him off your back for now, but if you can find something that points him in the right direction, don't hold back. Show him you're cooperating and not hiding anything. That'll divert attention from you and your team, and he'll be able to point his resources in the right direction. Understood?"

"Yes, sir. I'll make nice."

Morrison chuckled. "I'm not saying you have to French kiss the man, but you might have to pucker up and kiss his ass a bit."

Leroux grunted. "I'm not sure which image is worse."

Morrison tossed his head back and laughed, smacking Leroux on the shoulder. "Neither visual is particularly appealing, is it? Now, get to work. I've got thousands of assets out there getting more desperate by the minute."

"You don't have to remind me, sir. Two of the most important people in my life are up shit's creek right now."

Kane's Off-the-Books Operations Center

Outside Bethesda, Maryland

Mai stepped into the room, yellow rubber gloves up to her elbows, her hair tied back in a bun. "When was the last time you pigs cleaned this place?"

Tommy glanced over his shoulder at her. "Hey, don't blame me. I've only been here a few times."

"Yeah, and have you ever cleaned anything?"

He hesitated to answer, knowing it might mean a toilet brush getting shoved into his hand. "I'm sure I've done something."

"Uh-huh. Just like at home."

"Hey, you said you liked cleaning."

"You're lucky I do." And she did. Every time she was cleaning their apartment, she happily hummed away, scrubbing with a passion, as she liked to say. "Any luck?"

He nodded as he returned his attention to his station. "I've managed to hack a few cameras around the shop that are using cloud storage with compromised passwords. Looks like Dylan was planning on this day happening, so he did most of the legwork for me."

"So, did you find her?"

"Yeah. She was led out in handcuffs a few minutes after Dylan escaped and was put in the back of a police vehicle. I traced it to the Beijing Municipal Public Security Bureau. It's a local police station, though Dylan's database indicates it has a Ministry of State Security office in it."

"Do you think they'll be able to get her out?"

"I don't see how. Hopefully, Fang can get that intel to Leroux. You'd have to think if the CIA knew what this was about, they'd help him."

Mai leaned against the wall of the storage container. "But is *this* what it's all about?"

His eyes narrowed. "What do you mean?"

"I mean, rescuing her isn't the mission. It's Dylan's mission, but not the Agency's. The intel was the mission, if I'm interpreting things correctly. If the Agency finds out what he's trying to do, they might actually want him to stop. Rescuing her could create an international incident."

Tommy paused, facing her. "I never thought of it that way. But does it matter?"

"What do you mean?"

"I mean, rescuing her is the right thing to do, and Dylan's going to try whether the CIA agrees or not. It's our job to give him the best shot at succeeding until somebody tells us otherwise."

Mai stared at him. "What if somebody does tell us otherwise?"

Tommy tensed at the question and its implications. "I don't know. I think unless it were Chris or Fang, I'd tell them to go to hell."

Mai frowned. "Just remember, those you're telling to go to hell might have guns."

Inova Fairfax Hospital
Falls Church, Virginia

Tong scarfed down her lunch, starving. She was feeling remarkably well considering everything that had happened to her, and she attributed that to a number of factors. Leroux had essentially confirmed he had feelings for her, Nathan had declared them in writing, but also, she was determined to get back to work. The Agency was in trouble and her duty was to be there so she could help get to the bottom of what was going on.

An orderly entered the room and smiled. "Someone was hungry."

She groaned. "You have no idea. Can I have more?"

He chuckled, checking her chart. "Well, Oliver, you've got no dietary restrictions according to this. Just be careful, though. You were on anesthesia. Some people find they can't keep food down."

"All the more reason to bring me round two."

He laughed, policing her tray. "Round two coming up."

She leaned back and rubbed her stomach. She wasn't normally a big eater, but all the excitement had built an appetite and she needed her energy. She had to get herself back in fighting form because she wanted back in.

There was a tap at the door and she looked up, a smile spreading at the sight of Fang sneaking into the room. "What are you doing here?"

"Breaking the rules." Fang held a finger to her lips. "Let me speak before they kick me out." She held up a USB key then pressed it into Tong's hand, closing the fingers around it. "This is from you know who. It's the intel he was sent to retrieve. The op has gone to shit. The shop was hit and the asset's wife has been arrested. They're now in hiding, planning a rescue. We need this intel in Leroux's hands."

"What is it?"

Fang shook her head. "It's incredible if it's true."

"Can you tell me?"

"No, the walls might have ears, but let's just say that if it's true, the impact on China could be massive."

Tong frowned. Her heritage was Chinese, but she was American born and raised. She felt an affinity for the people of China, but in no way supported their government. "This impact, good or bad?"

Fang shrugged. "It could go either way, but it's critical Chris gets that. It could be what this is all about."

"You mean Sierra Protocol?"

"Yes. If the Chinese knew this intel was in play, they'd do everything they could to get their hands on it, even if it meant burning their entire network to the ground."

Tong's heart rate monitor beeped a little quicker. She was dying to know what the intel was, but Fang was right, the walls could have ears.

"So, can you get that into Chris' hands?"

"Yes, but it might not be until tomorrow."

"That'll have to do. I have a copy of it. I'm going to be swinging by home to leave him a note that it's urgent he contacts me."

"Will you be at your apartment?"

"No, our friend needs our help so I'm heading back. You know where?"

"Yes, I just wish I could help."

Fang smiled at her and patted her hand. "You just worry about getting better." She gestured toward the flowers sitting on the ledge. "Roses. Interesting. Who are those from?"

Tong's cheeks grew hot. "Um, a friend."

"Chris?"

A nervous laugh escaped. Did Fang know about their feelings for each other? If she did, would she tell Sherrie? "No, it's somebody I met on the bus."

"One red rose. I think he likes you."

Tong giggled. She desperately wanted to talk to Fang about Nathan, but she couldn't. Fang was part of the inner circle, and while Tong was within that group's circle of trust, Fang was Sherrie's best friend, and the girlfriend of Leroux's best friend. She could never confide in Fang her conflicted feelings about Leroux and this new man in her life.

Fang took her hand, clasping it in both of hers. "Go for it. Chris will always be there."

Tong inhaled sharply, her stomach in knots. "I-I don't know what you mean."

Fang smiled and patted Tong's hand. "That's fine. You don't have to say anything." She tapped Tong's other hand gripping the USB key. "You just make sure you get that to Chris." She nodded toward the flowers. "And give that guy a chance. You deserve to be happy. Now, I have to head back and try to save my boyfriend from my former colleagues."

Fang left the room and it took a few moments for Tong to notice that the monitor she was attached to had her heart rate up at least ten points, and she cursed. It was a human lie detector, and if Fang had any doubts about her suspicions, they were gone now. She sunk into the bed, closing her eyes as she sighed heavily, letting her mind drift to the handsome Nathan. There was no doubt he was interested, and as more time passed, especially since the flowers had arrived, any doubt she had as to whether she was interested was slowly falling to the wayside.

She had to give him a chance. They might go out for coffee and she could discover that he was an asshole, colossally stupid, or a political extremist. But he could turn out to be an intelligent, funny, rational man, and exactly what she needed in her life. Even if it weren't to work out, it would break the cycle she had been trapped in for years. Her heart needed to focus on a new target, even if that target might break her heart down the road.

At least her love for Leroux would be a thing of the past.

And the thought broke her heart.

Chan's Safe House
Beijing, China

Kane stood back and watched as the high-tech piece of machinery printed a face mask that would fool any facial recognition system. He glanced over at Chan. "I can't believe you have one of these. You realize how classified these are?"

"Clearly it was a good thing that I stole it."

Kane had to agree with his friend's assessment. But if Langley ever found out that this piece of tech was sitting in a converted garage in the middle of Beijing, they would be having a conniption fit, and would likely mount an op to retrieve it. While it didn't function in the same way as Mission Impossible's Hollywood creation, the end result was as equally good and had been in use for decades by the CIA. He had used its creations himself on countless occasions, and tonight it just might be the key to saving Bing.

Chan stood in front of a nearby mirror, turning to his side and rubbing his pot belly. "Not exactly the trim figure the People's Liberation Army likes to recruit."

Kane chuckled. "You're going in as a colonel. They're more forgiving of the higher ranks letting themselves go a bit."

"Yeah, but I'm too old for this."

The machine beeped, indicating it was done, and Kane gently removed the face mask, helping Chan apply it. Kane stepped back, his head slowly shaking, never ceasing to be amazed at the end result. "Too old, my ass." He stepped out of the way so Chan could see himself in the mirror, and the old man gasped, gently stroking his cheeks.

"I look twenty years younger."

"You do. When we rescue your wife, she's going to want to jump your bones."

Chan grunted. "That woman always wants to jump my bones. I thought when we got old, I'd be able to take it easy, but that woman…" He smiled. "What a woman."

Kane chuckled, well aware of her appetites and her constant teasing of wanting to sleep with him. When he and Fang were their age, if they were half as happy as these two appeared to be, he'd consider it a successful life.

Chan pointed at the machine. "Let's get yours going. Every minute we waste is a minute she's in their hands."

Kane loaded the parameters for his new face and inserted a fresh materials cartridge before activating the device. He wagged the empty box that had held the compounds necessary to create the mask. "How many more of these do you have?"

"Enough."

"Enough?"

Chan smiled. "Two years ago, Langley thought there was a chance I might be compromised, so they ordered me to destroy the machine. I brought it here along with all the cartridges I had. Then when that turned out to be bullshit, they sent me a new machine, and ever since then, every resupply after it's used, I request a couple of extra boxes. We both could have a different face for every day of the week if we wanted." He patted his own cheek. "Let's just try not to destroy them when we take them off." He dropped his jaw, forcing it from left to right. "It's remarkable. The longer I wear it, the longer I see it in the mirror, the more it feels natural."

"Eventually you'll forget you're wearing it, but you have to be careful. It's the simple things that we take for granted that can give you away. The nose that's itchy is not the nose the world sees. Scratching at this stuff can tear it apart."

"What if I have an itchy nose?"

"Don't scratch it. Squeeze your nose on both sides and give it a very slight wiggle, and try to do it when someone's not looking directly at you. You should practice that." Kane headed over to a nearby table. "All right, let's go over these plans. When we go in, we need to look like we know exactly what we're doing. We're going to have only one shot at this."

Beijing Municipal Public Security Bureau
Beijing, China

Duan cringed at a woman crying out in pain, begging for her torturers to stop. It could have been his imagination, but he could swear it was his grandmother. It wasn't a young voice. The door to the interrogation room had been intentionally left open, no doubt so he could hear what he had in store for him, or worse, what his family had coming if he didn't cooperate fully.

His entire family had been loaded into the back of a police transport while he had been put into the back of an unmarked SUV. He had been taken to the Beijing Municipal Public Security Bureau Headquarters where the Ministry of State Security had offices. He had read many interrogation reports over the years from beatings administered within these walls, perhaps even this very room. Everyone that worked here was well aware of what went on, and were all zealots, including those who wore police uniforms.

While innocent men at times entered, when they left, they were all guilty in the eyes of the state, signed confessions the proof. Nobody could take the pain they were willing to inflict here. They would eventually get the truth out of him no matter how much he resisted. And that fact begged the question, should he give in immediately and avoid the pain, or hold out as long as he could manage to give Kane a chance to get away?

A man stepped through the door, perhaps thirty years old, wearing a sharp business suit and a Communist Party pin. These were the ones you had to worry about—young, eager to advance, and completely indoctrinated. No mercy would be shown if this was whom they were sending in to discover what he knew. It suggested to him the Party had already decided what answers they wanted, they already had a version of the truth and they were going to beat him into giving it, the actual truth be damned.

The man closed the door then took a seat, placing his briefcase on the table between them. He said nothing as he opened the case, removing a laptop and a tablet computer. He opened the laptop then activated the tablet, tapping at it before finally staring directly at him. "I am Senior Investigator Pan. You are Mr. Duan, Domestic Intel Review Section Head at the Ministry of State Security."

"Yes."

"That wasn't a question," snapped the young man. "You'll only speak when spoken to, and you will answer all of my questions completely and honestly."

"Yes, sir." Duan squirmed, in desperate need of a bathroom break. This wasn't going to go well. "Sir, my family?"

"In a room at the end of the corridor. How they are treated depends entirely on you. Now, your job is to review interrogation reports that the system has flagged for human analysis."

He wasn't sure if he should answer, as it didn't sound like a question, but to be safe, he nodded. A file folder was removed from the briefcase and flipped open. His interrogator spun it around and pushed it across the table.

"Do you recognize this?"

It only took a moment for him to realize it was the debriefing transcript that he had passed on to the Americans. "I believe so. I think I reviewed it a few days ago. It should be in the system."

"It is, and you're correct. You did review it. Four days ago to be exact, and you flagged it as not requiring follow-up. Why did you make that assessment?"

"I assume you've read it."

"I'm the one asking the questions here. Why did you make that assessment?"

"Because it's nonsense. It's clearly the ravings of a lunatic or someone who's been beaten so mercilessly he's telling his interrogators what he thinks they want to hear in order to make the torture stop."

"A perfectly reasonable explanation, one that sounds well-rehearsed to me."

Duan's bodily functions threatened to break free from his control. "Look at me. I'm clearly terrified. I can assure you, if I had rehearsed anything, I wouldn't be remembering it now. I'm telling you the truth. You've obviously read it. You can't possibly think what the man said is true."

The tremor in his voice grew with each word spoken as the young man continued to just stare at him with a slight smirk. Oh, how he wished he lived in America where he could reach across the table and smack the smug smile off the kid's face. Yet perhaps that was just the movies, propaganda to show how lawless their enemy was, where violence was a solution to everything. The state-sanctioned news constantly reported on mass shootings in America, innocent people slaughtered by the thousands including children. He didn't buy it. Sometimes those behind the propaganda machine became overzealous and oversold their message. There was no way any civilized country would allow such things to happen.

Yet the footage looked so real.

"Who are you to dismiss this as nonsense? When somebody makes a claim such as this about the president, don't you think the Party should be made aware?"

He had prepared himself for this type of question. "I'm the section head. I was given the power to decide what should and shouldn't be sent up the chain. I decided it was nonsense. If I had then sent it to my director, then more eyes would have seen the nonsense and it might have been given credence the further up the chain it went. Something tells me the president wouldn't have wanted the dozens of eyes between me and him to read what that transcript says. If I was mistaken in my belief, then

I truly apologize, but I felt it was best to simply flag it as not needing to be followed up on and leave the allegations buried."

"You do agree what this transcript suggests is troubling?"

He had to be very careful here. He was being baited. You never spoke against the Party, and you certainly never spoke against the president. Not this one. "Not at all, because it's a fabrication. If for a moment I thought there was anything to it, I would have passed it on."

"Oh, I think you did believe there was something to it and you did pass it on." Pan tapped at his tablet and showed him a photo of Kane arriving at the airport. "Do you recognize this man?"

Duan leaned forward, squinting. He had rehearsed a story that he would give if ever confronted with something showing the two of them together. But that wasn't what was happening here. That photo could come next or it might not come at all. An idea occurred to him. His jaw dropped and he gasped, jabbing a finger at the photo. "That's the man from the Palace!"

"What?"

"He came up to me and asked me to take his photo at the Forbidden Palace earlier this evening."

"What were you doing there? Why weren't you with your family?"

Duan shifted in his chair. "I'd rather not say."

"You'd rather not say? I don't care what you'd rather."

This was a question he had rehearsed and could remember. He sighed. "Fine. As I'm sure you're aware, since you've read my file, I'm up for promotion. I desperately need it. It would mean easier hours so I could spend more time with my family. My mother isn't well and my wife suffers from sciatica. My eldest daughter has had a second child now that the restrictions have been lifted, and the demands at her job mean she and her husband need help with the children. I went to the Forbidden Palace to rub the knobs on the door for luck."

Pan frowned, leaning back and folding his arms. "You want a promotion yet you believe in such superstitions?"

"Now you see why I didn't want to say. I guess I can forget that promotion."

His interrogator leaned forward, swiping his finger across the tablet, flipping it around to show a video of the earlier encounter with Kane. "As you can see, we were already aware that you met the man. Do you know his name?"

"He never mentioned it."

"His name is Dylan Kane. He claims to be an insurance investigator for Shaw's of London."

"Claims?"

"We're quite certain he's an American agent, likely CIA."

Duan feigned curiosity. "If you know he's an agent, then why don't you arrest him?"

"You rarely arrest these people. You identify them then monitor them and see whom they meet with." Another swipe of the finger and a photo appeared, zoomed in on a pair of hands shaking. "This is where you handed him something."

Duan's heart went into overdrive and sweat trickled down his back. "I did no such thing."

The man zoomed in on the image, flipping it back around. "See the little black thing in the palm of his hand? It wasn't there when he reached out to shake your hand. That means you put it there."

The blood drained from Duan's cheeks. There was no denying what the photo showed. The USB stick he had handed to Kane was clearly visible. The angle suggested they had been under tight surveillance. The question was who had they been following? "I don't know what that is," he managed to force out.

"You put it there."

He vehemently shook his head. "You're mistaken."

"You continue to deny that you know this man?"

"I swear I don't know him. He approached me, asked me to take his photo. I did. Then he shook my hand. That's the first and last time I saw him."

"Interesting." The tablet was flipped around again and Pan tapped on the screen. He showed him the tablet, and Duan's eyes bulged at a photo of him and Kane together in Tiananmen Square from two months ago. "You don't know him?"

"That's right. I don't know him." Duan's voice was a mere murmur.

Pan swiped his finger over the screen revealing another photo of the two of them together that he recognized from six weeks ago. "Do you still claim to not know him?"

Duan closed his eyes, his shoulders slumping. They had been watching him for months, but it made no sense. Why? He had never passed anything on to Kane until tonight. This had nothing to do with the transcript he had stumbled upon. They had been watching him long before. The question was why? It was obviously because he was meeting with Kane. But how did they know? He had told no one, not even his wife, of what he was doing. The only other people who knew were on the American side of things. Was there a leak at the CIA? Or did they stumble upon him because his government was already watching Kane?

But if he had merely been caught up in routine surveillance of a possible foreign operative, how had they been able to act so swiftly tonight? And why? He had had any number of meetings with Kane over the years, yet tonight they decided to pick him up. Was it because they just got lucky with the photograph? He doubted that. Since nothing had ever been passed between the two of them previously, there would have been nothing to catch in any photographs. But this all happened very quickly. He had shaken Kane's hand, passing the intel, then gone directly to his car and headed home. Yet the authorities had already been in his apartment. The timing just didn't work. They had to have already been in place, waiting for the signal. There was no way routine surveillance took the photo, analyzed it frame by frame to see the handover, then sent a team to his apartment before he could even get there.

He supposed it was possible, but the timing would have to be near perfect, and he just didn't see it happening. They were already watching him. They were already anticipating the handover, and they already had the teams in place to take him down.

It was over.

"Do you have something to say?"

Duan sighed. "How did you find out?"

"I'm the one asking the questions here."

Duan opened his eyes and stared at Pan. "If you want me to cooperate, then you'll be answering my questions as well. I just want to know how you found out. There's no harm in telling me. It's not like I'm ever getting out of here."

Pan sneered at him. "Very well. We've known about you for some time."

"But why now?"

"I think you know why."

"The transcript?"

"Exactly. As soon as you saw it, you arranged an unscheduled meeting."

"But how could you know?"

Pan smiled and leaned forward, staring directly into Duan's eyes. "You don't think moles are the exclusive domain of the Americans, do you?"

Operations Center 2, CIA Headquarters
Langley, Virginia

Child pushed back from his keyboard, sending his chair into a spin as he stared up at the ceiling. "I think I might have found something."

Leroux turned. "What?"

Child dropped a foot, ending the spin. "I've been looking at the transmission logs like you asked me to, and I noticed over the past two months there have been these odd spikes. They only last about a second or two, and sometimes they're minutes apart, sometimes hours, sometimes even days. Security flagged them, but they haven't been able to determine the source. They're encrypted and are going out over the cellular network. Each burst is too short for a trace, and according to the report, whatever device is sending them turns itself off immediately after the transmission is sent."

Leroux folded his arms, leaning back. "That sounds odd. But why haven't we heard about it?"

"It looks like it's part of the mole investigation."

"It might explain why we've had people crawling through the ductwork for the past month or so," said Danny Packman.

Leroux had seen the teams going through the building, but he had seen things like that since he started here. Quite often, they were just routine, internal security doing their due diligence.

Child shrugged. "It might, but that's not what's important. They missed something."

"What did they miss?" asked Leroux.

"The opportunity to employ genius."

Everyone in the room groaned as Child spun with a grin. "That's right, people. Genius." He tapped at his keyboard then indicated the displays at the front of the room. Leroux turned to see a graph showing a series of spikes over a two-month time period. "Each one of those spikes is a data burst, sort of how we communicate with our satellites. We encrypt everything, compress it, and fire it up in a single burst. It's more efficient, less chance of failure, and unless someone has the decryption key, completely secure. So, that's what I assume is going on here, but they couldn't find the pattern. But they didn't know what they were looking for. We do."

"We do?" asked Leroux.

"They were looking for a mole, but they had no way of knowing who of the thousands of people in this building it could be. We know. Casey is the mole. So, I pulled up her security logs." He tapped several keys and a series of light green and red zones superimposed over the chart. "Green is when she was in the building. Red is when she wasn't. Notice anything?"

Leroux shook his head slowly as his jaw dropped. "Every one of those data bursts happened while she was here."

"Exactly. That's too much of a coincidence I would think, wouldn't you?"

Leroux had to agree. "So, if we assume she's the source of the transmission, how is she doing it? Every device in this building is registered, so it can't be a cellphone or anything like that. She had to have somehow got a device in here past security."

"Not only that," said Child, tapping his desk. "She had to get the device in *here*."

"You mean she was transmitting from in here? How can you possibly know that? And how could she have done it? These rooms are shielded. Everything goes through isolated transmitters and every signal is matched. Anything that doesn't match is flagged."

"Exactly." Child worked his station and light purple bands appeared over the graph, almost every burst contained within the purple zones.

"What am I looking at?"

"The purple is when she was actually in an ops center."

"Well, then, that doesn't make sense. How the hell could she transmit from in here with the shielding? That would mean she'd be in here and whatever was transmitting was outside of the room."

"There's one thing you're forgetting."

"What? Because I'm not a genius?"

Child grinned. "Your words, not mine."

Leroux twirled his fingers. "On with it."

Child jerked his chin toward the door. "Every time that door opens, there's a brief window where a signal can be transmitted."

Leroux turned toward the door, a lump forming in his throat. "Don't tell me."

Child's fingers tapped at his keyboard behind Leroux and the display updated, a series of narrow blue bands appearing, overlapping perfectly with almost every single burst detected. "I cross-referenced the security logs for the doors of each of the operations centers she was working. When the door opened, the device would transmit. All it takes is a couple of seconds."

"But how would it know?" asked Packman.

Child faced the analyst. "It's not really that difficult. It's probably passively scanning, and if it detects either a signal it's looking for, or simply other stray signals, it knows it can transmit. So, the door opens, signals from outside that door make it into the room, the device picks that up, fires its burst of traffic then shuts itself down immediately, probably before the door even closes. Our internal scanners are specifically set up so that when the door opens, new signals are ignored until the door closes again."

"Ignored?" asked Leroux.

"Well, ignored but logged. Otherwise, every damn time someone opened the door, the alerts would be coming on that there was an unauthorized transmission in the room."

"That's one hell of a security hole," muttered Packman.

"No shit," agreed Child. "When this is all over, we need to figure out a solution."

Leroux had already come up with a solution—double doors, like a pressure hatch on the space station. But that was unimportant now. What Child had uncovered sealed the fate of Casey's reputation. There could be little doubt now that she indeed was the mole, and it was heartbreaking. What had gone so wrong in her life for her to betray her country?

He faced Child. "When did these transmissions start?"

"About two months ago."

"All right, get all this info over to Team Two for verification. Then write an executive summary for me to bring to the Chief and Neary. We need to show progress and prove that we're actually working to find out the truth." He rose, heading for the door. "Send it to my phone. I'm going to go see the Chief."

Child nodded, attacking his keyboard. "You got it, boss."

Leroux opened the door, glancing up at the door frame, shaking his head at how a security hole that should have been obvious had been sitting right in front of them for years.

Chan's Safe House

Beijing, China

Kane fit his mask in place as Chan inspected a set of IDs that had just dropped into the tray from the laminator. Kane pinched at the nose, adjusting the fit. "I've always thought Asian men had a certain dignity to them." He still found it odd to see the reflection of a man who bore absolutely no resemblance to him mouthing his words.

Chan glanced over at him. "I always knew you were horny for our women. I didn't know that included our men as well."

Kane laughed and turned to Chan, straight-faced. "You know it was always you that attracted me, never your wife."

Chan stared at him, slack-jawed, then tossed his head back, roaring with laughter. "I'm telling her you said that. It'll break her heart. She'll probably never have me wear that mask we made of you again."

Kane gave him a look. "Huh?"

Chan grinned. "You should see the one I made for her."

"You two are messed up." Kane double-checked the mask was secured properly then brushed his hair and inspected his suit. "This fits perfectly."

"It should. It was meant for you. You'll be happy to know that you haven't put on any weight in the past two years."

"Good thing you've been stealing from the Agency for years, otherwise this op might not work."

Chan handed over the set of IDs for Kane's cover. Kane checked them, already having memorized the pertinent details. He was a Deputy Director at the Ministry of State Security. The face matched the data Langley had on file for the man, and the ID security features would pass any scan, matching the Ministry of State Security files exactly, the man's identity borrowed by another operative just last week, Chan wisely saving the particulars.

Kane faced Chan. "You ready?"

"Yes."

"And you understand what'll happen to us if we're caught?"

Chan gave him a look, pointing at the mask he wore. "This might make me look like I was born yesterday, but these old bones have been here twice as long as you have been, and I was born here. And what they'll do to us is what they're probably already doing to my wife, and the longer we sit here debating the obvious, the longer she suffers."

Kane bowed slightly. The man was right. No one understood more what was at stake than Chan.

They headed for the door and an uncertain future. The chances of this working were slim, and if they were caught, because of the nature of the intel, they would be tortured to reveal anyone they had passed it on to, then would be executed. There would be no prisoner swap. They were either rescuing Bing tonight, or dying trying. There was no middle ground here.

The stakes were simply too high.

Director Morrison's Office, CIA Headquarters

Langley, Virginia

Leroux reviewed the executive summary that Child had put together of his findings as he waited for Morrison to finish up a phone call. Neary sat in a chair beside him, apparently still bearing a grudge, as the man hadn't said a word to him, instead merely sporting a scowl the entire time. Morrison hung up the phone and smiled at them both. "Who knew Washington would be so concerned that all its spies were taking a day off?" He turned to Leroux. "I understand you have something?"

Leroux wagged his phone. "I've had the details sent to both your accounts, but my team has uncovered something I thought you should know about immediately."

"What have you found?"

"A series of burst transmissions, most of them sent from within operations centers manned by Casey."

Neary snorted with derision. "That's not possible. All traffic is monitored and those rooms are shielded. Any attempt at a transmission would have been detected and an alert sounded."

Leroux wanted to punch the man in the throat. "Well, fortunately, my team isn't as narrow-minded as some."

Morrison gave him a look.

"There's a security flaw."

"Nonsense. I helped design those protocols myself," said Neary.

Leroux ignored him. "We believe that Casey carried a passive device that would scan for new stray signals that would enter the room every time the door opened. When it detected those signals, it would send a burst transmission then turn itself off. The design of the security for the OCs intentionally turns off the alerts for any new signals detected while the door is open. The burst transmissions were logged but no alerts were ever sent, and security investigating them never determined the pattern of the transmissions because they didn't know who they were trying to match them against. Since we knew Casey was likely involved, we were able to match all of the transmissions to times when she was in the building, and most of them for when she was in an operations center, the transmissions coinciding exactly with when the logs show a door was open."

Morrison pursed his lips. "So, you're saying then that she was definitely involved."

"I'm afraid it looks that way, sir. I can't think of any other explanation."

Morrison turned to Neary. "What do you have to say about this?"

Leroux finally looked at the man and was immensely pleased to see the shocked look on the arrogant son of a bitch. "I'm not sure what to say."

"Well, you could say whether you agree there's a security flaw in your design."

Neary reluctantly nodded. "It would appear so. We're going to have to figure out a way to plug it."

"Double doors," said Leroux. "Like an airlock."

Neary's eyes slowly widened. "That's perfect." He inhaled deeply then extended a hand to Leroux. "I owe you an apology, young man."

Leroux shook the man's hand. "Don't worry about it. I was a bit of an asshole."

Neary chuckled. "My favorite type of people." He wagged the phone, Child's summary on the screen. "I'm going to have my people go over this, but I think it's pretty clear that Casey was definitely involved. We still need to find that device and determine who her handler was."

Morrison leaned forward. "Good. Now that we're all getting along, maybe we can start to make some rapid progress. Like you said, we need to find that device, because if it's still transmitting, even with Casey dead, we're still compromised. When was the last time it transmitted?"

Leroux brought up the logs. "Yesterday morning, just before she left the ops center at the end of her shift."

Neary's fingers drummed on the arm of his chair. "Did it ever transmit when she wasn't in the building? Even once?"

"No. The overlap was perfect."

"That means she took it with her at the end of the day."

Leroux smiled slightly. "So then it's in her house."

Neary shrugged. "It makes sense, doesn't it? I suppose she could leave it here and activate it when she got in and then deactivate it when she left at the end of the day."

Morrison wagged a finger. "Wait a minute. That wouldn't make sense."

"Why not?"

"Well, it's sending a burst transmission. That means it's recording data. The fact that it's transmitting from within an ops center has to mean she wasn't uploading data to it. Somebody would have noticed. It must have been recording whatever was being said in the room and then transmitting that whenever it had the opportunity."

Leroux's head bobbed. "That makes sense."

Neary leaned on one elbow. "Actually, it doesn't. Why wouldn't she just record everything then transmit it when she got home?"

"Because then the Chinese or whoever's behind this wouldn't be able to take advantage of the live intel. Too many of our ops concern them and they know it, so they would want whatever they could get as soon as they could get it so they might be able to act on it."

"There's still something not making sense here," said Neary, leaning back and folding his arms. "This report you sent indicates an awful lot of transmissions over the past two months. Some are within the ops center, some outside, but all within the building. And the frequency I'm seeing here suggests every time the door opened a transmission was sent, which has to mean it was automated."

Leroux regarded him. "Right. Your point?"

"Well, that's awfully risky, isn't it?"

"We did catch the signals."

"Yes, they were flagged, but no one ever thought they were coming from inside one of the ops centers, they just assumed they were stray external signals. If these had been properly looked into, like your team finally did, we might have tracked her down long ago. If I were her, I would only want to transmit when I had something worth transmitting to limit my exposure."

"What are you suggesting?" asked Morrison.

"Could she have not known?"

Leroux's eyebrows shot up. "You mean something was planted on her and she's actually innocent?"

Neary shook his head. "No, I can't see how she's innocent. After all, she'd have to be bringing this intentionally to and from work every single day. But she might not have known how it worked. She could have been told to bring it with her and just ignore it."

Morrison leaned forward, resting his elbows on the desk, steepling his fingers in front of his face as he tapped his chin. "Interesting, but it would have to be something that security would miss every single day. Something that it would be believable for her to bring into the room every shift."

Neary flicked his hand. "You've seen some of the stuff we've come up with. I have no doubt the Chinese can as well. And remember, who knows what smarts they built into it? It might not activate for ten minutes after each movement it detects, there might be a GPS in it that once it detects it's at Langley, it shuts everything down for half an hour. There are a million ways they could have countered our security. All they had to do was disguise it well."

"Piece of jewelry?" suggested Leroux.

"No, it would need to be bigger. Remember, this thing is transmitting."

"Sewn into her clothing?" suggested Morrison.

Another head shake. "When's the last time you saw a woman wear the same clothes every single day?" Neary rose. "With your permission, I'm going to go and start reviewing security footage. This all started two months ago. If we review the video from around that time, maybe we'll get lucky and see something that changed."

Morrison waved his hand toward the door. "Go. The sooner we find the transmitter, the sooner we can lift Sierra Protocol."

Neary hesitated at the door. "Sir, just because we find the transmitter doesn't mean this is over. We still don't know who her handler is and whether others have been compromised."

"True, but I think we can agree that her handler isn't in this building."

"Probably not, sir, but I wouldn't rule it out."

"Yet the likelihood of him being here yesterday, despite us suspecting we had a mole, didn't affect the operations of this agency. I've got thousands of assets out there, a hell of a lot of them American citizens that work for this government, that I have a duty to protect. Until Sierra Protocol is lifted, I'm not able to do my job. And you're forgetting one thing."

"What's that?"

"If he was satisfied with verbal or written reports delivered after the fact, he would have had no need for Casey to transmit. And the biggest risk at the moment is live intel getting out. Once we find that transmitter, we plug that hole, and any breach would be after the fact, which would greatly reduce the risk to our people."

"Unless there's another mole with another transmitter."

Leroux smiled as Morrison wagged his finger. "You're forgetting that we now know what to look for. The first time we see a burst transmission, we know we've got another problem. All we need to do is sync it to a door opening at one of our ops centers and the suspect pool becomes very narrow."

"You're right, of course. I'm a little too close to the problem, I guess." Neary opened the door. "I'll keep you posted." He looked at Chris. "Both of you."

Leroux acknowledged the courtesy and Neary left, closing the door behind him.

Morrison regarded him. "What are you thinking?"

Leroux scratched his chin. "Nothing."

Morrison eyed him. "Bullshit. What's that famous gut of yours telling you?"

Leroux sighed, leaning forward, resting his elbows on his knees, his hands dangling between his legs. "It's what Neary said. He's right. The number of transmissions is risky. If the Chinese were smart enough to design something that could fool our security, that she would be bringing in and out of the building every single time she was here, surely they'd be smart enough to build a switch into it. If she's wearing it, it could be as simple as tapping her watch, pinching an earring, any number of things that nobody would think twice about if they saw her doing it. Even if they saw her doing it repeatedly, it'd be chalked up to an affectation."

"Maybe they're not as smart as you think they are."

"Oh, I think they're smart enough. And if they aren't, they'd have stolen a design. Remember, these are the same guys that were smart enough to hide a chip behind another chip on motherboards that were sold by the thousands in the West. They can definitely create some sort of hidden switch."

"So then, what are you saying?"

"I have a funny feeling she had no clue."

Morrison leaned back. "I know she was a colleague of yours, Chris, and perhaps even a friend, but she killed herself, left a note implicating herself, and the logs don't lie. I think it's more likely that her handler didn't trust her to actually transmit, so she was given a device that removed the decision-making."

Leroux frowned. Morrison was right. He was grasping at straws because he couldn't believe someone he had known for so long could betray them all, putting the lives of people they were responsible for in jeopardy. If he could misjudge her, if he could misread her, who else was he wrong about? He rose with a sigh. "You're right, sir. We're going to follow the evidence, no matter where it may lead."

Morrison regarded him. "And remember that. No matter where it leads."

Inova Fairfax Hospital

Falls Church, Virginia

Tong climbed back into her bed, refusing to relieve herself in a bedpan. If she intended to return to work, she had to be able to take care of herself, and one of the most basic needs a person had was the ability to go to the bathroom where God intended.

On a toilet.

She had managed, though her shoulder wasn't happy about it, and she babied it as she positioned herself, waving off any help from the concerned nurse.

"You don't have to be a hero."

"I'm not trying to be a hero, but the longer I can't work, the more lives are put at risk."

The nurse frowned at her. "Living in this city, I've learned not to bother asking what people do for a living when they talk like that. I'm sure the Agency can live without you for a week."

"A week?" Tong laughed. "There's no way in hell I'm waiting a week. I intend to be at work tomorrow."

It was the nurse's turn to laugh. "What you intend and what will happen, I think, will be quite different. You rip those stitches, you'll be right back in here."

Tong gestured at the IV still in her arm. "Am I on any painkillers?"

"Yes."

"How strong?"

"Strong enough that it's letting you do things you shouldn't."

"Cut it in half."

"What? You'll be in agony."

"Maybe, maybe not. But we'll never know, will we, unless we try."

"I'll have to talk to the doctor first."

"You do that, and tell him I want to speak to him as soon as possible."

The nurse turned toward the door. "Oh, where'd this cutie come from?"

Tong looked toward the door. A teddy bear sat on the table holding a small red velvet box. "When did that get here?"

"If you don't know, then I certainly don't. Someone must have delivered it while you were asleep." She picked it up and brought it over, giving him a squeeze. "He's so cute."

Tong smiled, her problems momentarily forgotten. She pulled the card out from the red bow around his neck and flipped it open.

Sonya,

I saw this little guy when I was buying your flowers. I was going to bring him tomorrow, but couldn't wait.

Nathan

P.S. You're a cute sleeper.

Tong smiled and the nurse regarded her. "Another love letter from the hero?"

She nodded. "What do you know about him?"

"Nothing. Apparently, he's the guy who put an end to things, but he's refused to speak to the press."

"So, he's not a glory hound."

"Apparently not. The only thing he seems to care about is you. You're a lucky woman."

Tong sank back into the pillows, holding the bear to her chest, the small box digging into her skin. She opened it and giggled. Inside were two miniature teddy bears, one in a blue ribbon, one in a pink, their paws sewn together, and he had used a marker to put an N on the boy bear's ribbon and an S on the girl's.

She held it up for the nurse to see, and she laughed as she headed for the door. "Oh, girl, you've either got the most romantic man in the world or the cheesiest. Either way, he could be a keeper."

"Maybe." She rolled onto her side, closing her eyes, and hugged the bear, a smile on her face as her heart raced with the excitement of a teenage girl. And prayed these romantic overtures were those of a confident man merely wanting to make it clear to her that he liked her, rather than a desperate man chronically single for a reason. Whatever his flaw was, she just hoped it was something she could live with, because she was tired of being alone, tired of pining after Leroux, tired of living life at a standstill. Her eyes grew heavy.

She was just tired.

Beijing Municipal Public Security Bureau

Beijing, China

Kane had found the key to success in any Hail Mary operation such as this was confidence. That confidence didn't have to be genuine, merely projected. He was quite confident this plan was going to fail and that he was going to die a horrible death. But to the outside world, he was supposed to be there and listened to, though actually, that was Chan's role. He was doing all the talking, and it was odd to see the voice he had known for years coming from a face two decades younger.

The young officer behind the desk reviewed the piece of paper Chan had handed him. "I'm going to have to have this verified, sir. I've received no word about a prisoner transfer."

"You do whatever you need to do, Lieutenant, but in the meantime, take us to her."

"I'm afraid I can't do that, sir. She's in interrogation now."

Kane took an intimidating step forward, having said nothing since walking through the door.

Chan held a hand out, stopping him. "Lieutenant, I'm not going to tell you who this man is. You don't want to know who this man is. It terrifies me that I know. If he speaks, then it's too late for you. He works for the Ministry of State Security, Special Division."

The lieutenant's eyes bulged. "Special Division?"

"Yes. You know what that is?"

The young man nodded.

"Then you know whom he reports to directly."

"The-the president?"

"Exactly. So, who do you think sent him here?"

The lieutenant gulped, setting the forged transfer order aside. "Come with me." He rose and buzzed them through, then led them to a side door. He swiped his pass then pulled open the door after a click sounded, a small red light in the scanner turning green. He led them down a long corridor, numbered doors on either side, some open, some closed, shouting, crying, screaming heard the entire way.

This was everything the reports had indicated.

The briefing notes Kane had read on this place indicated it was where the Chinese took locals for interrogation. Foreigners were taken elsewhere and treated quite differently, the torture more psychological than physical. Here, however, where they didn't care about some foreign government or Amnesty International complaining, the gloves literally came off.

A woman's voice cried out and a pit tortured his stomach as he recognized it as Bing. Chan inhaled sharply but maintained his cover as they continued to follow the lieutenant down the corridor. The young man stopped in front of a door. "She's in here, sir."

Kane had been paying attention to the markings on the doors, each interrogation room paired with an observation room. He pointed at the door, giving an inquisitive look to the lieutenant, who shook his head, rapidly answering before Kane used any words, no doubt remembering Chan's warning.

"I don't think there's anyone observing, sir."

Kane flicked a finger at the door and the young man swept his pass then pushed the door aside, revealing an empty room with a two-way mirror exposing the horror on the other side. Kane pushed the young man through the door then followed him in, Chan on his heels.

"As you can see, sirs, there's your prisoner. Like I said, she's been under interrogation since she arrived. Do you want me to interrupt them?"

Kane reached out and snapped the man's neck, gently lowering the body to the floor. He removed the man's pass as Chan stared through the glass, grimacing as his beloved wife was mercilessly beaten. Kane drew his weapon and fit a suppressor in place. "I'll do the shooting." He opened the door, finding the corridor clear. He took several steps to the interrogation room, swiped the confiscated pass, then pushed the door open. He stepped inside, putting two rounds in each of the men responsible for this atrocity.

Chan rushed past him as Kane closed the door, retrieving the men's wallets and IDs. They might prove useful later, and Langley was always eager to get their hands on the latest paperwork, just in case new security measures had been implemented.

"Please stop, please," sobbed Bing.

Chan dropped to his knees in front of his wife, taking her hands. "It's me, my love."

Bing wept. "Oh, no, they got you too?"

"No, I'm here with a friend. We're getting you out of here. Can you walk?"

She sniffed, staring at the disguised man through swollen eyes. "Is it really you?"

"Yes. Can you stand?"

"I don't know."

"Well, let's try." He took her hands and lifted her to her feet. Her short legs wobbled and she nearly collapsed.

"I'm sorry, Husband, I can't."

"Then I'll carry you."

Kane glanced over at them. There was no way Chan could carry his wife very far. He handed his spare weapon to the man. "You know how to fire this?"

"Of course."

"Then don't, unless it's absolutely necessary." He kneeled in front of Bing, pressing on her ribs. "Can you breathe?"

Bing nodded.

"Tell me if it hurts. Keep breathing as deep as you can."

She did as told and Kane completed his inspection of her rib cage. Nothing appeared broken, a couple of winces suggesting she might have bruising. The key was her ability to breathe and tolerate the pain she was about to endure.

"I'm going to carry you over my shoulder. It's going to be uncomfortable. It might hurt a bit where your ribs are bruised, but it means we get out of here in sixty seconds. Are you good with that?"

"Just don't touch my bum too much. You might make my husband jealous."

Kane grinned at her then exchanged a relieved smile with Chan. That was the woman he had come to know over all these years, her sense of humor wonderful. He patted her cheek gently. "I don't know. It's a wonderful piece of ass. I might not be able to help myself."

She giggled. "Husband, leave us."

Chan rolled his eyes. "I'm beginning to regret I came here to save you."

"To save my wonderful ass."

"Are you ready?" asked Kane.

She nodded.

"Okay, here we go."

He picked her up and slung her over his shoulder. He handed the pass to Chan who opened the door.

"We're clear." Chan held the door aside as Kane rushed through, sprinting down the hall, Chan on his heels covering their escape. Poor Bing whimpered with each step, but it would soon be over if they could just get through this door before someone noticed them on the cameras.

They reached the end of the hallway and Chan scanned his pass. The door clicked, the indicator changing to green. He pushed the door aside.

An alarm sounded, somebody having spotted them. Chan hopped over the half-height wall as shouts erupted. Kane twisted, propping himself up on the edge of the gate, swinging his legs over.

"Halt!" shouted someone behind them.

Chan spun, raising his weapon. He fired two shots and Kane cursed as four men emerged from the opposite side of the reception area, toting Type 81 assault rifles. He took them out with four practiced rounds. Chan tried the doors but they were locked. Kane fired several rounds into the glass but it merely splintered.

"Assault rifles."

Chan rushed over to the tangle of bodies. He grabbed one of the rifles and tossed it to Kane then retrieved one for himself, spraying gunfire at the security personnel scrambling into action. Kane emptied the mag into the lock, weakening the mechanism, then booted it several times before it finally gave way. Chan continued to fire, screaming in rage at what had been done to his wife, before tossing the spent weapon aside.

He followed Kane through the door and they sprinted across the parking lot. Chan opened the back door of the rental Tommy had arranged for them. Kane gently placed Bing in the back then Chan climbed in with her. Kane slammed the door shut then jumped behind the wheel. He started the car then put it in gear, hammering on the gas, firing several rounds at the door as security personnel finally dared to pursue them.

He blasted through the gates, the guards chasing after them briefly. He lost them in the light overnight traffic of Beijing. They only had minutes to switch vehicles before the extensive camera network picked them up. He glanced in his rearview mirror. "How's she doing?"

"She's alive."

"Give her the Tylenol."

Chan cursed, apparently having forgotten they had prepped for this possibility. He grabbed a bag from the floor as Kane guided them toward their transfer point where Tommy would override the cameras, creating a dead zone.

"Two minutes."

"Copy that."

Kane checked the mirror to see Chan holding a water bottle to his wife's lips as she swallowed down the painkillers. They had stronger stuff than Tylenol, but they couldn't risk giving her anything without knowing the true extent of her injuries. Hopefully, in less than an hour, the edge would be taken off her pain.

Kane tapped his phone, sending the prearranged signal to Tommy who, if he was doing his job right, would disable all the cameras for the second time tonight. He entered the China World Mall and descended into the underground parking. He parked on the second level then helped Bing out, carrying her to their transfer vehicle, this time cradling the tiny woman in his arms. He glanced down at her battered face and wished he had been able to make those responsible suffer more than the double taps had. At least they were dead, so they couldn't do this to anyone ever again.

Unfortunately, there were millions more indoctrinated into the Party's way of thinking that would take their place. China already was the dystopian future portrayed in too many movies, and had to be stopped before they became too powerful. Right now, their only Achilles heel was their economy. If the West could divest itself entirely from the Chinese economy, the world might stand a chance.

He grabbed the keys he had left behind the tire in the event they all hadn't made it out, then helped Bing into the back seat. Within minutes, they were back onto the streets of Beijing, heading for a final transfer point, the flashing lights of police cars and other security vehicles, most heading toward the chaos they had left behind, keeping his pulse pounding. It was only a matter of time before roadblocks were set up, and it was a miracle they had gotten this far. He just prayed that things continued to break their way.

He had no desire to die in China.

Beijing Municipal Public Security Bureau

Beijing, China

Duan flinched at the blaring of an alarm, followed soon after by several popping sounds. Pan sprang from his chair and hauled the door open, disappearing into the corridor as more gunshots rang out, confused shouting joining the cacophony of sounds. Something was going on, something completely foreign in China. He could see people assaulting a police station in America, but not here. It had to be a rescue attempt. It had to be Kane coming for him, but there was no way in hell he was leaving without his family.

He rose and peered out the door. Several people were poking their heads out like he was, fear in their eyes, the braver ones heading toward the fight. He sucked in a breath and squared his shoulders.

Act as if you're supposed to be here.

He stepped into the hall and strode in the opposite direction of the gunshots, his jaw clenched, a scowl forced where a trembling lip demanded to be. A few people glanced at him, but nobody said a word.

153

He stepped aside as two armed men raced past him. He reached the end of the hall and opened the door to his right, crying out in relief at the sight of his family cowering on the floor. His wife rushed into his arms and he held her tight.

"Is everybody all right?"

Tearful heads bobbed.

"Good. Now, I need everybody to be brave, everybody to be quiet, and everybody to do exactly what I say. We've only got a couple of minutes at most. Understood?"

More head bobs.

"Then follow me." He poked his head out into the corridor, finding all attention still directed toward the gunshots. The door to his right burst open and someone rushed through, sprinting toward the front of the building. Duan caught the door before it closed, then beckoned his family through, cringing at every whimper, at every sniffle. He gently pressed the door closed behind them and looked around.

They were in an office area, but no one was in sight. The gunfire from the front had stopped, so they didn't have much time. He spotted an exit sign and led his family toward it, pushing open the fire door. An alarm sounded but it was drowned out by the security siren. He led them out the back of the building and toward the street, uncertain as to where to go, but certain he had to get as far away from here as possible then contact Kane.

Only the Americans could help them now.

Kane's Off-the-Books Operations Center

Outside Bethesda, Maryland

Fang opened the door to Kane's operations center. "It's just me!" she announced, sealing them back inside. "Any word?"

Mai poked her head around the corner, flashing her a smile as Tommy replied. "We're still waiting to hear."

Fang hung up her jacket and joined the couple in the nerve center of the off-the-books complex. "Waiting to hear what?"

"Whether or not they're still alive."

Fang cursed. "Are you telling me they went in?"

Tommy held up his hands. "Hey, don't shoot the messenger. Chao didn't want to wait and frankly, I don't blame him. If it were Mai, I'd have gone in." Mai squeezed Tommy's shoulder and he reached up, patting her hand.

Fang sighed as she dropped into one of the spare chairs. "You're right. I was just hoping to get back before they started the op. What's the last communication we have?"

"The second signal to take down the cameras in the parking structure where they were did the first switch."

Fang smiled. "Really? That means they survived the rescue."

Tommy scratched his chin, folding his arms. "Hopefully, but we don't know who sent the message and how many were in the car."

"Can you check the cameras?" asked Mai.

"No, I disabled them, remember?"

She smacked her forehead. "Sorry. This spy stuff is all new to me."

Fang crossed her legs under her. "The next phase of the extraction was to switch vehicles again."

"Are there any cameras there?" asked Mai.

"No, it's a dead zone, which is why it was chosen." Fang checked her watch. "If they're on schedule, they should be approaching the next transfer point within a few minutes. That's the key one. If they can make it past that point, they should be free and clear."

"Let's hope so," sighed Mai. "I don't think my heart can take much more of this."

Fang chuckled. "This is nothing. Just imagine if you were listening to it live, or worse, watching it. There's nothing more exciting or nerve-racking or terrifying when it's people you care about."

Beijing, China

Kane turned right, heading toward their most critical exchange point. He glanced over his shoulder at Chan. "Time for you to come up front."

Chan leaned forward, picking up a pair of six-inch stilts that he described as the most torturous device ever invented by man, though the sometimes-necessary pain was worth it, since it added half a foot to his height and would eliminate him from most suspect pools if the police were searching for a six-foot tall man.

He held one up against the window as he pretended to take the second one off, then tossed them both on the floor of the back seat. The idea was that they wanted at least one camera to have seen him handling them. He climbed forward and dropped into the passenger seat as Kane made a left.

"Are you ready for your big reveal?" Kane asked, and Chan grinned at him, the effect disturbing, since the man had changed his disguise before they left the garage and was now wearing Kane's face.

"Goodbye, my American stud muffin."

Both Kane and Chan laughed at Bing's joke. Chan reached up and carefully removed the face, just in case they might need it again, then dropped it in his lap, turning his face from side to side slowly, pretending to stretch his neck muscles out, but in reality giving good profile shots to any cameras within range.

Kane wanted the Chinese to think that any footage they had of him might actually have been Chan in disguise. His friend being identified was no longer an issue. There would be no doubt in the Chinese authorities' minds who rescued Bing, a rescue where a dozen uniformed officers were killed or wounded. Chan was dead if he stayed in this country. Their end game had them escaping back to the United States, though that was only going to happen if Sierra Protocol was lifted.

But that was the next problem.

Internal Security Center, CIA Headquarters

Langley, Virginia

Tanner stared at the security footage of Casey, watching for any differences but still spotting nothing. She loved being the leader of Echo Team, though it could be quite boring at times, considering the CIA rarely operated on American soil, so she had jumped at the opportunity to help analyze footage.

Michael Lyons, her second in command, snapped his fingers, jabbing at the screen. "There!"

"What?"

"Her briefcase."

Tanner leaned forward and cursed. "How the hell did I miss that?"

"You've been too busy admiring her outfits."

She gave the man a look. "Since when have you ever known me to be concerned about fashion?"

"Hey, I never said you were concerned. In fact, most of the things I've seen you wear, I'd look good in. When someone asks me what it's like to have a female team lead, I just laugh and say, 'Tanner's a woman?'"

Tanner chuckled, though deep down was hurt. Just because she had a job that was traditionally a man's didn't mean she wasn't a woman. On the job, she wore what any man would, merely because it made sense. Dealing with skirts and blouses and pantyhose and other such nonsense was too impractical for a job that could demand she be in a gunfight half a second from now. She wore pants, shirts, sneakers, whatever allowed her to do her job as well as any man, if not better. But when she got home, in the privacy of those four walls, she loved stripping out of her boring things and slipping into something feminine, whether that was a little black dress for a night out with friends, or pink silk pajamas with bunny slippers for curling up on the couch with a glass of wine and a Bachelorette marathon.

"Hey, I was just joking. You know I'd never say anything like that."

She flinched, not realizing she had lost herself in a moment of self-pity. She gave him a weak smile. "Don't worry about it."

He leaned closer, lowering his voice so the others in the room couldn't hear. "Remember when you were at the Palladium last week?"

Her eyes narrowed. "How the hell do you know I was there?"

"Remember the guy who wolf-whistled at you?"

She leaned away from him. "Wait a minute. That was you?"

He grinned. "Yep, but once I realized it was you, I took a dive under the table."

She laughed, remembering the incident vividly. It had made her feel good. She had been out on the prowl with a couple of her friends, looking to burn off steam, and when she had walked through the door, that whistle had thrilled her.

"You still got it," her friend Mary had said as they made their way to the bar, all eyes on them, but no one approaching claiming ownership of the catcall. She had been a little disappointed, but had still hooked up with an on-again-off-again friend with benefits. She wasn't looking for a relationship, just a stress reliever.

She gave Lyons a look. "Whistle like that again at me and I'll rip your tongue out."

He stuck it out at her and her hand darted forward, grabbing it, his eyes bulging at her incredible reflexes. "I'm thorry," he said, and she let go.

She returned her attention to the screen, zooming in on the briefcase. "Bring up the day before."

Lyons tapped at his workstation and froze the image, expanding the frame. "See? Different."

"Bring up yesterday."

Lyons did, quickly confirming she was still using the new briefcase.

"Fifty bucks says that whatever we're looking for is built into that briefcase."

"I'd take that bet, but I'm not stupid," replied Lyons as he rose. "Let's go get our smoking gun."

Xiangheyuan Subdistrict

Beijing, China

Kane pushed the manhole cover aside then checked in all directions to make certain no one was watching. They were in a camera dead zone, but there still could be locals about, though at this hour in China, most people who wanted their state-assigned social credit score to remain high didn't want to be seen on the streets in the middle of the night.

"It's clear. Let's get in as quickly as we can."

Kane, still wearing his disguise, scrambled out then reached down, lifting Bing out of the storm drain and onto the street. Chan climbed up sans disguise as Kane retrieved the keys to their final transfer vehicle and unlocked the doors, helping Bing inside. Kane handed the keys to Chan who got behind the wheel.

"Good luck. I'll make contact in the morning, assuming I'm still alive."

Chan laughed as he pulled a ball cap down low that had been sitting on the passenger seat, fitting a fake beard in place and specially designed glasses that appeared to spread the eyes apart, screwing up most of the facial recognition points that might be used if you were caught on camera. "I'll see you tomorrow."

Chan pulled away and Kane tossed his weapons and anything else incriminating into the drain before dragging the manhole cover back into place. He walked briskly down the road, and within a few minutes, spotted Xu's idling SUV. He tapped on the rear quarter panel so as not to terrify the man. The door unlocked and Kane climbed in the back.

"Thanks for coming out so late."

"No problem," said Xu as they pulled away from the curb.

"Do you have what I asked for?"

"In the bag beside you. Hotel?"

"Yeah. Just obey all the speed limits. We don't want to draw any attention." Kane opened the bag and pulled out a tube of bright red lipstick. He removed the cap and twisted the tube, exposing the colorful substance, then smeared some across his cheek and lips. He put the cap back on and returned the tube to the bag, then pulled out his handkerchief. He ran it over his cheek and lips, doing a poor job of removing the lipstick, then returned the now-stained monogrammed cloth to his pocket. He retrieved a small bottle of perfume and sprayed himself a couple of times with it.

"Oh, my God, this stuff is awful!"

Xu snickered. "You said you wanted cheap perfume. That's my sister's."

"The public shouldn't be subjected to shit like this." Kane mussed up his hair and undid the top three buttons of his shirt. He pulled out a bottle of Beluga Gold Line vodka. "Nice choice."

"I figure the girl's wearing cheap perfume but you're drinking nothing but the best."

"You got that right." Kane took a swig, swishing it around his mouth before swallowing, then poured some in his hand and ran his fingers through his hair then over his face and exposed chest. He took a couple more shots before recapping the bottle and returning it to the bag. He pulled out a small rectangular device, removing the cap. He held it up so Xu could see it in the rearview mirror. "Is this preset?"

"Yes. I selected the World of Suzie Wong nightclub. It's high-end and popular with foreign businessmen looking for easy women. It's known for being discreet with no cameras. I've already selected the black light stamp. Just put it on the back of your left hand."

Kane pressed the end of the device against his hand as instructed then pushed down, the device capable of leaving any ink or ultraviolet stamp from any number of locations. He recapped it and tossed it into the bag, zipping everything up. He handed it forward and Xu took it, placing it in the passenger footwell.

"As soon as you drop me off, dispose of that safely. That includes the vodka. No one will believe you were able to afford that, not on what I apparently pay you."

Xu grinned. "You could always give me a raise."

"I suppose I could. If I survive the next few days we'll discuss it."

"That bad?"

"The insurance industry can be pretty rough sometimes."

Xu laughed. "I have no doubt. We're almost there."

"Okay, good. Now, remember your story. You picked me up at the hotel, took me to the Forbidden Palace, then to the market. I spoke very little except to give you the destinations. You thought I might be coming down with a cold because my voice sounded a bit different. When I didn't return from the market, you went home, then you got a call to pick me up, just as you did. You picked me up just where you did, then dropped me off at the hotel and went home. They'll probably ask why you didn't think it was strange that I didn't come back from the market, and you're just going to shrug and say you've worked for me for many years and it wouldn't be the first time I had met a woman and decided to wine and dine her. Your instructions were always to just head home if I wasn't back within an hour and not to worry about it. The key thing to remember, but don't stress it too much, just make sure you mention it at least once, is that when I first got in the vehicle at the hotel my voice sounded different, but when you picked me up tonight, everything was back to normal."

"Gotcha. Don't worry, Mr. Kane. It won't be the first time I've dealt with the police, and I'm sure it won't be the last."

They pulled up in front of the hotel and Kane reached forward, squeezing the man's shoulder. "Good luck."

"You too."

Kane stumbled out, making a show with his balancing act. A doorman rushed down and helped him up the steps. "Thank you, young man. You're a scholar and a gentleman."

"Are you all right, sir?"

"My heart's broken. One of your country's lovely young ladies let me buy her drinks all night then sent me back to my hotel rather than home with her."

"Well, sir, if it's companionship you're looking for, perhaps I can arrange something."

Kane batted his hand. "Don't bother. I'm just going to go up to my room, take a piss, vomit, then pass out, all on the toilet." He snickered at his own joke as the man handed him off to another hotel staff member. As he was led through the lobby, two men in suits rose, intercepting them on their way to the elevator.

"Mr. Dylan Kane?"

Kane twisted his head up to look the man in the eye and squinted. "Have we met?"

"You'll be coming with us, sir."

Kane dropped to the floor then released his bladder, capping his Oscar-worthy performance. He just hoped they let him change his pants.

Being interrogated while reeking like urine was not his idea of a good time.

Operations Center 2, CIA Headquarters

Langley, Virginia

Leroux looked up as Neary entered the operations center, a smile on his face as he triumphantly held up a briefcase.

"We found it."

Leroux leaned back. "So, that's the briefcase she started using two months ago?"

"Yes, and the Chinese are getting pretty damn good at their job. All the electronics are hidden in the latches that are platinum plated. The plating will show up on our scanners at security, but it looks like it's just part of the design, not some sort of shielding. This metal trim here doubles as the antenna."

"I assume you've got it disabled?"

Neary tapped the case. "We found the power supply and have removed it. We're going to be analyzing it in a shielded room to see exactly how it functions."

"Where did you find it?"

"It was in her Agency-issued safe. It had a few secure documents in it, all properly logged out."

Leroux pursed his lips as he regarded the case. "So, a woman who's betrayed her country and committed suicide follows Agency protocol right until the end?"

"It appears so. It does make you wonder what was going through her mind."

"What does this mean for Sierra Protocol?"

"I've asked the Chief for twelve more hours. I want all three shifts rotating in while we watch for any data bursts. If we go twelve hours with nothing, then we're lifting Sierra Protocol."

Leroux cursed. "A whole lot can happen in twelve hours, especially in our business."

"Agreed, but at least now we know she was the mole and how she was transmitting. We still need to figure out who gave her this briefcase, but at least now we know when. Trust me when I say I'm not going to rest until I find out who her handler was and how he was able to convince her to betray her country."

Leroux regarded him. "So, you're starting to have your doubts too?"

"Oh, I have no doubt she's the traitor, but everything about her suggests it's completely out of character. I think the Chinese had something on her, something compromising, and used it to blackmail her into cooperating, and then she finally had too much, couldn't take it anymore, but rather than turn herself in she killed herself. Any luck on your end?"

"No, beyond the data bursts, we haven't found any other evidence of a breach. No patterns of unusual activity where she was involved. As far as we can tell, she just did her job and did it well. But while she was doing that, that briefcase was transmitting everything that was being said around her. We're putting together reports on all the missions that might have been compromised. We might have to burn some assets, extract some. The consequences of this are huge, but in twelve hours at least we can start to take action."

Neary headed for the door. "I look forward to reading your report."

"As do I," said Leroux with a smile.

Neary opened the door then indicated the frame. "I'll be putting in your recommendation for double doors on all the ops centers. A brilliantly simple solution to the problem."

The former rival left and Child grunted. "Who knew you two would become bosom buddies?"

Leroux chuckled. "When you become more senior, you'll learn that when you're young, respect is earned, not granted by those who are older than you. But just remember, it goes both ways."

"How's that?"

"Older people shouldn't assume you don't know what you're talking about because you're younger, but younger people shouldn't assume that older people are out of touch. The Chief might not know all the latest buzzwords and tech, but his over three decades of experience more than makes up for it."

"Yeah, but the Chief listens to you."

"And why do you think he does?"

169

Child shrugged. "He's a smart Boomer?"

Packman groaned. "Every time I hear that term it pisses me off. Most people using it have no clue what a Boomer is. The Chief is Gen X. At the top end of it, but still Gen X."

Leroux chuckled. "Very top end. Just remember, Gen Xers and Boomers and those that came before them are who built this nation into the greatest country in the world. And while our generations might like to think they've got a lock on what's right, they have to remember that women's rights movements and gay rights movements and all these movements that they've embraced, including environmentalism, all began before they were born. And it was the efforts of their parents and grandparents that gave them the life they have today. The Chief listens to me because he recognizes through experience that he doesn't know everything and that he doesn't need to know everything. That's why you have subject matter experts that make sure he knows what he needs to know in order to make an informed decision.

"Now, I'm going to stand down our side of the team and have Marc's continue for four hours. Get some rack time and be prepared to relieve them so everybody gets some rest. In twelve hours, everything comes back online and we're going to find out what kind of shit shows are happening all around the world. Whatever sleep you can get tonight might be it for the next few days." He started packing up his stuff. "I'm going to go see Sonya and see how she's doing."

Inova Fairfax Hospital

Falls Church, Virginia

"So, what's the word, Doctor?"

"Everything's looking good. The stitches are holding, there's no bleeding, all your vitals are perfect. How are you holding up with your pain meds halved?"

"It's throbbing a little," replied Tong. "But it's not too bad. I'd rather keep my mind sharp."

"Your mind being sharp is one thing, but suffering for no reason is another."

"While I would normally agree, my pain and discomfort are irrelevant. I'm desperately needed at my job."

"I'm well aware of where you work, and I'm quite certain whatever you do is very important, but sometimes you have to think of yourself."

"No disrespect, Doctor, but everything I'm hearing from you suggests my life is no longer in danger. I can't tell you what's going on, but believe me when I say I'm needed at my post."

The doctor gestured at the turned-off TV. "Then I take it you haven't been watching the news?"

"No, they kept talking about the shooting so I turned it off."

"Well, I don't know what's going on at the Agency, but your shooting story has been shoved to the back burner with all kinds of talking heads speculating about what something called Sierra Protocol is." Her eyes flared and he chuckled. "You may work for the Agency but you're no spy." He leaned closer, lowering his voice. "So, what *is* Sierra Protocol?"

"I'm sure I have no idea what you're talking about, but let me just say, if it's serious enough to be covered by the news, then it's serious enough for me to put up with a little pain and discomfort, don't you think?"

The doctor sighed. "I'm just a doctor. My concern is for my patients' well-being. I can tell you with confidence that as long as you take it easy on that shoulder for the next week, you're going to be perfectly fine. If you want to run off and do office work it will be against medical advice, however, you should be fine. I highly recommend that if you do check yourself out AMA, you put that arm in a sling and get yourself back here the moment you feel anything out of the ordinary. So, what's your plan?"

"I'm going to contact my supervisor and find out what's going on. Who knows? He might tell me just to go back to bed."

"Let's hope that's what he says. Even another twelve hours of rest could make all the difference."

There was a tap at the door and Tong smiled as Leroux poked his head inside.

"Is this a bad time?"

"Speak of the devil," she said.

Leroux grinned. "I've been called worse but not by better."

"Just give us a moment, would you?" said the doctor.

Tong batted her hand. "This is my supervisor and my friend. Anything you have to say you can say in front of him."

Her doctor faced Leroux. "If you're her supervisor, tell her you don't need her at the office. Sierra Protocol or otherwise, she needs supervised rest."

Leroux's eyes narrowed. "Sierra what?"

The doctor chuckled. "You're a hell of a lot better at this than she is."

Leroux laughed. "Doctor, she's the one that makes me look good to the bosses. So, what's this? Are you trying to fly the coop?"

"The doctor says it's safe for me to go back to work though he doesn't recommend it."

The doctor headed for the door. "I'll leave you two to discuss your sierras and tangos and whatever other phonetic alphabet protocols you've got going. From what they're saying on the news, I'd have to guess that sierra stands for shit-show, so I'll leave it in your hands to make the judgment call. Just remember what I said, young lady. First sign of trouble, you get your ass back here. Otherwise, what might have been a simple gunshot wound could turn into something far worse."

"Yes, Doctor."

The man left and Leroux pulled a bouquet of flowers from behind his back, a standard package no doubt from the gift shop downstairs. He glanced at the roses. "Huh, somebody's got me beat."

She giggled. "It's not a competition." She took the flowers. "These are lovely." She placed them beside her. "What can you tell me?"

"Well, he's not wrong, it is a shit-show, but we just don't know how much of a shit-show. The Chief's lifting Sierra Protocol in about eleven hours and then we're going to find out what's been going on with our operatives and assets around the world."

"How bad do you think it's going to be?"

"That all depends. Anything not compromised by Casey's breach should be fine. Our officers should have simply gone to ground, then should come out of their rabbit holes as soon as they hear from us. The bulk of our assets are rarely engaged, but anybody who was compromised, we have no idea. I'm concerned about—" He stopped. "We really shouldn't be talking about this here. The room hasn't been swept."

She was certain it was safe, but with everything going on, a little bit of paranoia might be a good thing. She gasped. "I almost forgot!" She retrieved the memory stick that Fang had given her from her bra. "A mutual friend wanted me to give this to you."

Leroux's eyes narrowed as he took it, and she could tell he was desperate to ask for details.

"My understanding is everything's explained on it."

"I guess I'm going back to the office then."

She smiled. "I wish I could go with you."

"And I'd love to have you there, but not a lot is going to happen until the protocol's lifted. You get your rest." He gave her hand a squeeze then held up the intel. "I'm going to go find out just what the hell's going on that has a certain someone ignoring Sierra Protocol."

Tong regarded him. "Are we sure that he's ignored it?"

"Consider who delivered it. There's only one way she could have gotten her hands on it. If he got everything set up and running so that he could transmit this, he must feel it's incredibly important."

Tong had to agree. "Not to mention he had her deliver it to me to get to you."

He removed his wallet and tucked the memory storage device inside before returning it to his front pocket. "Now, you get your rest. I don't want to see you until you're actually healthy. We can handle things. I'll see you later."

She squeezed his hand. Nothing could be better than being with him, but it was a lost cause. Her future lay elsewhere. She glanced at the teddy bear. Perhaps it lay with Nathan. "I'll see you tomorrow."

Leroux left and she rolled to her side, her back to the door, hugging the stuffed animal, her mind a jumble of conflicting emotions and desperate curiosity as to what was happening. If Sierra Protocol was to be lifted, then the Agency must have discovered something that indicated Casey was guilty, and now that she was dead, the risk was over. To think a friend could betray them all and give absolutely no indication, had her questioning everything. Was there anybody she could really trust? She sighed with the realization that due to the nature of her business, she could never truly trust anyone inside or outside of the Agency.

And that was soul-crushing.

Leroux stepped onto the elevator, battling the pit in his stomach. He shouldn't be jealous, yet he was. A dozen yellow roses with one red rose? A teddy bear? Tong had a boyfriend, yet why hadn't she mentioned it? The reason was obvious. She was moving on from her infatuation with him and had a private life she intended to keep private. That was fine. That was a good thing. Yet, he had to convince his heart of that. Perhaps part of him had always thought of her as his backup plan if something were to happen with Sherrie. If she were to finally realize that he was all wrong for her, Tong was always there in the wings, waiting. Now that was gone and it was a good thing. He'd have to keep repeating that to himself until he believed it, but for now, he had more important things to worry about.

What was this intel? The mutual friend was obviously Fang. Sherrie was out of the country, as was Kane, leaving Fang the only one Kane would trust to send the intel to. But if it was as important as they had been made to believe, he would never send it to her phone, even using the encrypted app, not without being certain she was in a secure location. It meant it had been sent to the servers at his off-the-books operations center. To transmit classified intel to an unsanctioned server had to mean it was either incredibly important, or Kane was in serious trouble and the intel was at risk.

His mouth filled with bile at the thought his friend could be in trouble. If it were anyone being affected by Sierra Protocol, it would be Kane. After all, if this breach did indeed involve the Chinese, he was a Chinese specialist, in and out of that country all the time. As was common practice by all governments, they would merely observe him in the hopes of finding out who his contacts were, and only take him down when it was absolutely necessary. If the intel now in his pocket were as critical as events suggested, the Chinese might have made their move.

Kane might already be dead, his network taken down.

Leroux checked his watch. There were still almost eleven hours to go before they would get any answers. The elevator doors opened to the parking level and he stepped out with several others. He headed for his car on autopilot, lost in his thoughts, ignorant of what was going on around him. He reached into his pocket for his key fob and pressed the button to unlock his car.

The lights flashed just ahead when a shoe scraped behind him. His heart leaped. It could be completely innocent, or it could be somebody who had witnessed the transfer of intel. He held in the panic alarm on the car. A couple of seconds later, the lights began flashing, the horn honking. He bolted toward his vehicle and grabbed the handle, yanking open the door. He climbed inside then pulled the door closed. Somebody grabbed it before he could shut it completely. He yanked on the door hard as he leaned his entire body to the right, jamming his key in the ignition as they yanked again, the car continuing to blare its horn. He shoved his foot down on the brake then pressed the button to start the car as the door was wrenched open, two hands reaching inside for him.

He shoved the car in reverse and lifted his foot off the brake. A fist struck his chin and he finally understood what it meant to have your bell rung. The jolt was jarring, disorienting, and he swore his ears truly did ring. But his foot was on the accelerator and the car continued to reverse as the man grabbed at him. Leroux's senses returned and rather than fight the man off as he had been trying, he grabbed the wheel and cranked it hard to the right as he continued to press on the gas, the backup camera giving him a clear view of what was behind him.

He pressed harder, the car racing backward, the man no longer attempting to get his hands around Leroux's neck, instead flailing for the steering wheel. Leroux raised his left hand, his fingers balled into a fist, and slammed down hard on his assailant's fingers. The hand broke free and Leroux quickly smashed the other hand. There was a yelp as his attacker fell clear of the car. Leroux reached out and grabbed the door, hauling it shut as he continued to reverse before hammering on his brakes as he reached the rear wall. He pressed the button, all four door locks clicking shut, his assailant on his knees in the headlights.

The exit was through this man.

He put the car in drive and floored it, aiming directly at his attacker, the engine whining as he rapidly gained speed. While he would love to kill the man, or at least wound him horribly so he could be taken in for questioning, it was evident more was going on here and it had to do with the intel in his wallet. It was critical he survived this and made it to Langley.

He gripped the steering wheel with both hands, locking his elbows, and roared as he aimed directly toward what had to be a Chinese operative. The man rolled out of the way at the last second and Leroux blew past him, racing toward the ramp at the far end. He lifted his foot off the accelerator, preparing to make the turn to safety when gunfire erupted behind him, his rear window shattering. He ducked, cranking the wheel hard as he slammed on the brakes then shoved back down on the gas, sending the car surging up the ramp and out of the line of fire.

The gate was just ahead but there was no way he was stopping for it. He braced himself once again. His bumper crashed into the barrier, the wood splintering away, the attendant shouting after him as he burst out of the parking lot. He cranked the wheel hard to the left, turning onto the street, checking his rearview mirror for any signs of pursuit, thankfully finding none. He had to get to the Agency no matter what the cost. He could deal with the consequences of his traffic violations later. He had to deliver this intel to the Chief. If the Chinese were willing to kill for it, it was obviously as important as they had been made to believe.

He eased his foot off the accelerator, relaxing the death grip on the steering wheel. He reached back and grabbed his seat belt, jerking it forward and passing the clip to his right hand. He flinched at a jolt of pain and looked down to see the right arm of his dress shirt drenched in blood. He gasped, letting go of the belt and it shot back into the holder with a snap.

When the hell did that happen?

It had to be a gunshot wound. There could be no other explanation. The brief scuffle couldn't have resulted in that much blood, not from a fingernail scratch. There was a good amount of blood now and he felt weak. He drew a deep breath, holding it. If he were bleeding out, he had to slow his heart rate. He had to buy himself time. He had to reach the Agency.

He reached forward, pressing the button to activate his car's voice features. "Dial the Chief." An error message displayed, indicating there was no phone paired. He slapped his hand against his breast pocket and cursed. His phone wasn't there. In the struggle, he must have either dropped it or the man had grabbed it. He cursed. It was unlikely the Chinese could crack it since it had Agency-level security on it, however, it meant he couldn't call for help, which might have been the more likely reason for the man attempting to get his hands on it.

His heart raced again as he checked his rearview mirror. His assailant had to know where he'd be heading, and if the man thought preventing him from making a call in that short time would be useful, it obviously meant he intended to pursue. He spotted a car well back, weaving between lanes, and it wasn't a Honda Civic driven by some Vin Diesel wannabe.

It had to be the Chinese.

He hammered on the gas, the small engine of his Toyota whining in protest before the automatic transmission dropped a gear and gave him some torque. The light ahead turned amber, then red, but he had no choice. He blasted through the intersection, horns blaring at him. "Sorry!" he shouted uselessly. He was doing almost sixty now in the city streets, his driving officially dangerous, but he had to reach Langley and he didn't know how much time he had left. His heart hammered from the situation and he gave up on steadying his breathing. His arm was drenched in blood, the crisp white shirt sticking to his pasty white arm. He checked his rearview mirror and he could see his pursuer, though he didn't appear to have gained, the chaos left behind at the intersection slowing him.

A siren squawked to his right as he blasted past a McDonald's. He checked his mirror to see a squad car pulling out onto the road, its lights flashing, its siren now blaring. He cursed, but kept his foot pressed to the floor. He had to think. He could stop and tell the officer what was going on and it could all get sorted out, the officer protecting him. But what was more likely to happen would be that he would stop, the officer would get out, and by the time Leroux was out of the car and in handcuffs, the Chinese agent would have caught up to them, shot the officer, taken the intel, then shot him.

No, he had to keep trying to get to the Agency and use the cop as a buffer between him and the Chinese.

It wasn't far now. The squad car rapidly gained on him, the officer far more skilled a driver than he was, not to mention the squad car was built for pursuit, unlike his modest Toyota. He was almost clear of the city, then it was a short jaunt up the George Washington Memorial Parkway to get to the CIA Headquarters complex. Unfortunately, it also meant the cop was liable to overtake him easily.

If only I had my phone.

He reached the parkway and continued to swerve through traffic, and he noticed with a smile that with the police officer on his tail, the cars ahead were taking notice and pulling out of his way. The pursuit was actually working for him. He continued to pick up speed, the miles to his destination rapidly ticking down. He had lost track of his pursuer, the squad car dominating his rearview mirror, and as long as it remained there, the Chinese weren't the issue. Once he was through the gates, nothing mattered, as the local police officer would have no jurisdiction on the federal territory.

The turnoff for the Agency was just ahead. He slammed on his brakes, killing his speed, and wedged himself between two cars then onto the shoulder, gunning it up the side. The squad car forced his way over, and like Lemmings, the cars ahead all moved to the left, freeing up the lane for Leroux. He came around the bend, the gates just ahead, cars lined up waiting to be cleared. He swerved over into the oncoming lane, gunning it toward the gate, a guard stepping out and holding up his hand then drawing his weapon as he saw the police car in pursuit. Leroux hammered on his brakes then put the car in park, jumping out and running toward the guard. He fished his ID out of his pocket, holding it up.

"I'm Chris Leroux, Analyst Supervisor! I report to Director Leif Morrison! I'm being pursued by Chinese agents! You need to let me through the gate before you detain me!"

The security officers at the Agency were second to none, and where at most places healthy skepticism might have resulted in him being told to freeze and get on the ground, he instead was ushered through as other security personnel raced toward the area. Leroux held up his hands as the squad car screeched to a halt on the other side of the barrier. He couldn't see the Chinese, but they could still be out there, preparing to take him out.

"You're wounded."

Leroux glanced down at his arm, completely drenched in blood. "Sniper," he managed to warn before dropping to his knees.

"Get him inside!" shouted somebody. "And call a medic!"

Arms grabbed him and he was lifted into the back of an SUV. Moments later, he was hurtling toward the safety of his second home. He grabbed one of the security people by the arm. "Get my wallet to the Chief."

Then he passed out, his mission accomplished.

Infirmary, CIA Headquarters

Langley, Virginia

Morrison sprinted down the corridor, his chest tight, his stomach in knots with worry. He had just received a phone call indicating Leroux had rushed through the gates then dropped unconscious from a gunshot wound, claiming to have been pursued by Chinese agents. His phone was pressed to his ear, Echo Team Leader Tanner at the other end of the line. "I want two guards on him at all times. And lock down his team. They were the only ones who knew he was going to the hospital. And I want a security detail on Tong. If it's safe to do so, have her transported here."

"I take it Sierra Protocol's not being lifted?"

Morrison grunted. "What do you think?"

"I think I'm canceling my plans for this evening."

"Probably a wise move. Get on it. Let me know when everyone's secure."

"Yes, sir."

Morrison ended the call as he reached the infirmary, two armed security on either side of the door due to the emergency situation. He showed his ID and was cleared through. Moments later, the woman manning the front desk looked up and smiled.

"How can I help you, sir?"

"I'm Director Morrison. You brought one of my people in. Chris Leroux."

The woman squared her shoulders at his title. "Yes, sir." She pointed down a corridor. "Room Two."

Morrison rushed in the indicated direction to find a room bustling with activity, two armed guards at the door plus several other security personnel in the room while a doctor and two nurses hovered around the bed, everyone chattering.

He growled. "Anybody who absolutely doesn't need to be in this room, get the hell out!"

The entire room spun toward him, the doctor among them. "Who are you?" she asked.

"Director Morrison."

"Thank God. Tell these people to get the hell out of my way. He's not exactly a threat."

Morrison jerked a thumb over his shoulder. "Everybody who's not medical, get out."

The head of internal security, Ken Crawford, stepped forward. "Sorry about this, Chief, I just got here and I'm still trying to sort things out."

Morrison pointed at Leroux. "He's one of my people. He's not a security risk. Let's discuss it in the hallway."

"Yes, sir but…"

Morrison held up a hand. "One guard. He keeps his mouth shut and stays out of the way."

"Thank you, sir." Crawford pointed at one of the men who crisply nodded, standing by the door as everyone else filed out.

Morrison stepped over to the doctor. "How's he doing?"

"Oh, he's fine. He got a pretty good graze on the arm. Deep. Sliced him right open so there's a lot of blood, and then from what I understand, he was in quite the chase here, so that got his heart pumping. That, combined with my belief he has an aversion to seeing his own blood, caused him to pass out."

Morrison smiled down at Leroux. "So, he fainted?"

"Pretty much. I'm just sewing him up now. He'll have a sexy scar for the ladies, but he'll be fine."

"Has he said anything?"

"He woke up a couple of times. What was it he said?"

One of the nurses responded. "'Chief' and 'wallet.' That was all I could make out."

"Where's his wallet?" asked Morrison.

The guard by the door replied. "On the table there, sir, with his other personal belongings."

Morrison stepped over and retrieved the wallet. He fished through it and found a USB key stuffed inside. He clasped it in his hand, returning the wallet to the table. "When he wakes up, let me know. And tell him that I got what he wanted me to have."

"Yes, sir."

Morrison stepped out into the hallway.

"Just what's this all about sir?" asked Crawford.

"I'm not sure yet." He held up the USB key. "But he almost died trying to get this to me. He's not a suspect, he's a hero, and you'll treat him as such."

"Absolutely, sir. But we will need to question him."

"No, you'll need to take a statement and I want to be there. When the doctor says it's safe for him to talk, you let me know, but no one talks to him before I do."

"Understood, sir."

Morrison headed toward the elevators, his mind racing. What was on this memory stick that was so important that someone would try to kill one of his best people on American soil? He needed to see what was on this, but he couldn't risk just plugging it into his laptop. He had no way of knowing if Leroux knew what was on it, and he couldn't dare risk the network being exposed to what could be a virus. It needed to be accessed from an isolated terminal by somebody who knew what they were doing, and someone he could trust.

The question was, who the hell was that? Was Casey the only compromised asset within the Agency, or were there more? Was Leroux targeted because of who he was, because he had visited Tong, or because somebody had handed him the memory stick? And who was that somebody?

He growled as he boarded the elevator. There were simply too many questions that desperately needed answering, and he needed somebody he could trust. Unfortunately, the two people he trusted the most, Leroux and Tong, were both out of commission.

He smiled.

There was one they both trusted, and that was too low on the totem pole for the Chinese to bother attempting to compromise.

Inova Fairfax Hospital
Falls Church, Virginia

Tong looked up as Tanner entered the room. The leader of Echo Team was familiar to her, though someone she rarely dealt with in person. The fact she was here meant something had gone wrong.

Horribly wrong.

When Leroux had been here earlier, he had indicated the Chief was lifting Sierra Protocol in less than eleven hours. If Echo Team was here, there was no way that was still true.

"What's wrong?" she asked.

Tanner swept the room before replying. "Chief's orders. He wants you transferred to headquarters immediately, assuming it's medically safe to do so. If not, we're to secure the room."

The heart rate monitor beeped a little faster. "What's changed in the past hour?"

"Leroux's been shot."

Tong gasped, her heart racing. Her eyes burned and Tanner quickly held up a hand.

"He's all right. Last update I had was he was already out of surgery. It was just a graze, a deep one. They stitched him up and he's going to be fine."

Tong collapsed back on the bed. "Oh, thank God. Just a tip, the next time you deliver news like that, you start with the fact that someone is okay before saying they've been shot."

Tanner chuckled. "Good thinking. I'll try to remember that."

Tong sat up and reached for her IV to tear it out when Tanner stopped her.

"Just a sec. We're waiting for clearance from the doctor, so just hold tight."

"I don't care what the doctor says, I need to be at headquarters."

"Trust me, I understand how you feel." Tanner glanced over her shoulder toward the door. "Mike, bag."

Another member of Echo Team stepped inside, handing over an empty duffel bag.

"Anything you want to take with you?"

Tong stared at her blankly, her mind completely preoccupied with the thought that Leroux had been shot.

"Sonya, snap out of it."

Tong flinched. "Sorry." She pointed at a nearby table where the staff had put all of her clothes and belongings inside a bag from when she had been stripped down for surgery. "I guess just that stuff."

Tanner grabbed it and stuffed it in the bag. "Anything else?"

Tong eyed the flowers from Nathan sitting on the ledge, then the other bouquet from Leroux sitting beside it in a pitcher provided by one of the orderlies that she was quite certain was meant for urine collection. Bringing flowers with her would be indulgent. "No, I think that's it."

Tanner jerked her chin toward Tong. "What about him?"

Tong looked down to see the teddy bear gripped tightly against her side. "Oh, I forgot. Yeah, I guess we can bring him." She handed it to Tanner and Nathan's gift was stuffed in the bag before it was zipped up.

Two nurses rushed in along with her doctor. He wagged a folder. "This is your file. Give it to the doctor on site. If he or she has any questions, have them call me day or night."

Tanner took the folder as the nurses unhooked Tong from the monitors and pulled the IV.

"Like I said, take it easy on that shoulder for as long as you can. Any problems, you make sure you seek medical attention. Understood?"

"Yes, Doctor. Thank you."

He smiled at her. "I guess you weren't kidding when you said they needed you. I hope whatever the hell this Sierra Protocol thing is, it all works out."

"So do I, Doctor."

"Okay, you're good to go," said one of the nurses.

Tong sat up, swinging her legs over the edge of the bed.

"Mike, body armor."

Mike stepped back into the room, handing over a vest. He gave the nurses a look. "Now I know how you guys feel in surgery. Scalpel, sponge, wipe my brow." He pointed a finger at Tanner. "If you ask me to wipe anything, I'm out of here."

The nurses giggled as did Tong, the break in the tension welcome. A wheelchair was brought in then Tong, now sporting body armor, was helped into it. Tanner handed her the bag with her belongings then turned to her subordinate.

"Is asking you to push her too much for you, or should I get someone else?"

"Fine, I'll push, I'll push. It's better than wiping."

"You'll be wiping my ass if you keep up the chatter."

"I'm sure that's harassment."

Tong gripped the bag tight to her chest with her good arm, the other throbbing as she was pushed into the hallway. Half a dozen men and women, fully armed and armored, made quite the spectacle as they escorted her to the elevator and eventual safety.

And she thanked God she was no longer hooked up to a monitor, because she was convinced she was more scared now than when she had been shot.

Operations Center 2, CIA Headquarters

Langley, Virginia

Morrison stepped into the operations center and found Randy Child sitting alone at his customary workstation, directly behind where Leroux would normally sit. He had ordered the young man escorted here, and the poor kid appeared terrified, his only company two armed guards.

"You, um, wanted to see me, sir?"

Morrison dismissed the guards. "Don't worry, son, you're not in trouble. The fact is, you're the only one I think I can trust with something."

Child's eyes bulged. "Sir?"

Morrison held up the memory stick as he strode toward Child's station. "Leroux almost got killed getting me this. I need to know what's on it."

Child gasped. "Is he okay?"

"Yes, he'll be fine."

Child leaned forward and took the small device, giving it the once over. "Looks like a standard USB key. Do we know what's on it?"

"Something worth killing for."

"So, we don't know if it's been booby-trapped?"

"No idea."

"No problem." Child slid over to another workstation then logged in, inserting the key into a reader then closing the lid, sealing it inside. "This machine is completely isolated from the network. No connections whatsoever, physical or otherwise. The reader is a Faraday cage, so if the device is designed to transmit when activated, the signal isn't going anywhere."

Morrison smiled. "I knew I came to the right person." He grabbed a chair and sat beside Child. "So, what have we got?"

"Looks like we've got a compressed file." Child double-clicked on it, bringing up the contents. "There's a series of images and a README document dated today."

"Bring it up."

Child opened the document and Morrison quickly read what turned out to be a brief letter from Lee Fang that had Morrison's pulse pounding in his ears. Kane was in trouble, Chan's operation busted, his wife arrested, and the two fools, rather than obeying Sierra Protocol, were planning to bust her out or die trying.

He glanced up at the clock on the wall. "This was from hours ago. Kane could already be dead, or worse." It was one line though that concerned him most.

The intel Kane was passed is shocking. I highly recommend you keep this as compartmentalized as possible, as the Chinese government will stop at nothing to contain this leak.

Morrison gestured at the screen. "Open up the first image."

Child brought up the first file and Morrison cursed. It was a photo of a computer screen, everything in Chinese. He glanced at Child. "You don't happen to read Chinese, do you?"

Child grunted. "For all I know, that's a recipe for Kung Pao chicken."

Morrison grunted. "So, it means as much to you as it does to me." He leaned back. "We need this translated, but it has to be by somebody we can absolutely trust."

"It's too bad Sonya's not here," said Child. "She reads Chinese."

Morrison smiled slightly. "She might not be here, but she will be shortly."

"Can we wait that long?"

"I don't think we have a choice. Somebody just tried to kill Chris to get their hands on this. Right now, we don't know whom we can trust, but I'm quite sure we can trust Sonya."

Child tapped the edge of his keyboard. "I could run it through the machine translator."

"How accurate is it?"

"Fairly, assuming it can visually pull the characters from the image. The problem with translating Chinese is that written Chinese isn't like English or French or Russian. It's more like reading hieroglyphs than Latin. You need a native Chinese speaker to really understand the nuances behind everything."

Morrison had heard enough. "Forget it. I can't risk the machine interpreting things one way, then acting on that. We need a native Chinese speaker like you said, and that's going to have to be Sonya." He reached out a hand. "Give me the memory stick and wipe everything from this machine."

"You got it." Child flipped the lid up on the reader and pulled out the USB key, handing it over.

Morrison rose and headed for the door. "Stay here and don't discuss anything that just happened with anyone except for me, Chris, or Sonya."

"Yes, sir."

"Chris is in the infirmary being stitched up. I've ordered Sonya brought in so that I can protect her. Once she's here, we'll take a look at those images again."

"Can I tell the others what happened to him and that he's going to be fine?"

Morrison smiled slightly. "Son, you're going to be in this room alone until I come back. Get comfortable."

Ministry of State Security Headquarters

Beijing, China

Kane sat in the chair he had been shoved into when he first arrived at the Ministry of State Security headquarters. This was the big time, and he had to play his part perfectly, otherwise, he was in for an unpleasant time before perhaps being executed. The best-case scenario, if he didn't pull this off, was that he'd be held and tortured for potentially years until an exchange was arranged. Perhaps the Chinese would be willing to trade him for one of their sports heroes naïve enough to get arrested with an illegal substance on them in a hostile country.

He had to hope all the subterfuge included as part of tonight's plan worked. Thankfully, when he arrived, they had made him strip out of his clothes and handed him a new set liberated from his hotel room, though not before shoving him in a shower. He had taken the opportunity to stage a rapid recovery from his inebriation. He couldn't risk them testing his blood alcohol level and discovering he was faking it. He had to cooperate just enough that they believed he was drunk, as opposed to pretending so he might evade their questioning. He now sat upright, pretending to be scared, drowning himself in coffee and Chef Kong biscuits.

The door opened and a man entered. "I'm Pan Shiying." The man sat, opened a briefcase, then removed several folders and a tablet computer. "And you are Dylan Kane, insurance investigator for Shaw's of London."

"That's correct," said Kane, careful to be obvious about choosing his words deliberately, as if forced to overthink things. "I think there's been some sort of misunderstanding. Is it because I was drunk in public? I'm sorry if I made a scene. I'm not usually like that."

"This has nothing to do with your drinking, Mr. Kane. In fact, I wouldn't be surprised if we tested you, we'd find you weren't drunk at all."

Kane leaned forward and breathed on the man then belched, saying nothing except giggling. "I'm sorry, this is serious. Ask me whatever you want. I've got nothing to hide."

Pan wagged the tablet. "We've got quite the file on you, Mr. Kane, if that is indeed your real name."

"So my mom and dad have told me."

"Or so your CIA handlers have told you."

Kane stared at the man incredulously then jerked back, feigning concern. "Wait a minute, you're being serious, aren't you?"

"Very serious, Mr. Kane. My government's been following you for some time. You're a frequent visitor to our country. Always flying in first class, chauffeurs everywhere, the finest hotels, the finest restaurants…and unusual friendships." Pan brought up a photo of Kane and Duan in Tiananmen Square. "You two seem fairly friendly."

Kane leaned forward and stared at the photo. "Why not? He's a friendly guy."

"So, you admit to knowing him?"

"Of course. That's Duan Guofeng. I met him a couple of years ago."

"Now, how did you meet a member of State Security in your line of work?"

"I didn't."

Pan regarded him. "What do you mean?"

"I mean, I didn't meet him with respect to work. I was here for work, but I met him at a noodle bar. I was having trouble explaining to the waitress what I wanted, and Duan here overheard and helped me. I asked him to join me and we shared a lunch together and had a delightful conversation. It was refreshing dealing with someone in your fine country that wasn't trying to deceive me. I've always thought the Chinese people were wonderful, but in my line of work, most of those I deal with are trying to commit insurance fraud or cover up their negligence. When you see that day in and day out, it sort of taints your opinion of a people."

Kane held up a hand. "I know it shouldn't. You shouldn't judge an entire culture by a few bad apples, but like I said, when almost all the apples you deal with are bad, it's easy to make that mistake. Duan, however, was just a genuinely friendly person. We talked about his family, his country, what life was like in Beijing. Don't worry, we didn't talk politics or anything like that. He had lots of questions about what things were like in the United States, about my job. We kept in touch over the years. I try to see him every time I'm in Beijing."

"So, you're telling me that a suspected American spy just so happens to be friends with a section head in the Ministry of State Security?"

Kane shrugged. "Actually, I had no idea he worked for the…Ministry of State Security, did you call it? I knew he had a government job, but he never really spoke about it, and I didn't pry. It's hard to know what to ask people in such a repressed country." He leaned forward, holding up a hand. "No offense."

Another photo was shown. It was from earlier when the handover had taken place.

Kane squinted. "When was that?"

"Tonight."

"Tonight?" Kane shook his head. "No, that's the Forbidden Palace, isn't it? I've been there before, but not tonight."

"So, you deny that this is you?"

"Definitely looks like me. Like, my God! They say everyone's got a twin in the world, so that must be mine. You're sure it's tonight and not another night? I can't remember if he and I ever met at the Forbidden Palace, but maybe we did over the past couple of years. Quite often we meet and just go for a walk. Sometimes you lose track of where your feet carry you."

"No, Mr. Kane, this was definitely tonight. You left your hotel, your driver took you to the Forbidden Palace, you pretended not to know Mr. Duan, had him pretend to take a photo of you, then when you shook hands, he passed something to you. You then left, got back in your vehicle, were taken to the Zhongguancun e-Plaza where you then went to Li's Photo where you evaded arrest until you showed up at your hotel pretending to be drunk."

Kane folded his arms defensively, turning himself slightly away from the man. "Listen, I don't know what the hell's going on here, but I know a frame job when I see one. Remember the business I'm in. People try to deceive me all the time. That is *not* me. I was *not* at the Forbidden Palace today. You said I used my driver to take me there. Well, ask him yourself. I told him to go home. I wouldn't need him for the evening. I decided to go out later because I was bored. I went to a bar, met a lovely lady, wined her and dined her, partied all night, and then she dumped me on the way out the door. I called my driver, he came and picked me up and brought me back to the hotel. End of story. I don't know what the hell this is that you're talking about, shaking hands, things being passed on, evading arrest. I think you're trying to trick me into some sort of confession."

Kane turned, staring at the camera. "You hear me, whoever's watching? I'm innocent. This man's trying to frame me. I want to talk to somebody from my embassy."

There was a tap on the door but it didn't open. Pan rose and leaned on his knuckles, staring at Kane. "We've tried this the easy way, Mr. Kane. When I come back, we'll be moving on to the hard way."

"Beating me to say what you want me to say doesn't make it the truth. I don't know what the hell's going on here, but I want to speak to somebody from my embassy. I have rights."

Pan smiled. "No, Mr. Kane, this is the People's Republic of China. You, an American, have no rights. I can throw you in a cold, dark cell for the rest of your life and there's nothing your country can do about it." He headed for the door then turned back one last time. "A lot of people are dead tonight, and somebody's going to pay. Your friends may have freed Chan Bing, along with Duan and his family, but nobody's coming for you here, Mr. Kane. There'll be no rescue. I *will* get the truth out of you."

Kane was elated to hear that Duan and his family had somehow escaped, and also pleased to hear they hadn't truly connected him to what had happened earlier. He kept his face neutral. "Then I guess we're both in for a long night, because you've already got the truth out of me."

Infirmary, CIA Headquarters

Langley, Virginia

Morrison stepped into the infirmary and the woman behind the desk shot to her feet, recognizing him. "He's in recovery. Room Six." She pointed down the corridor.

"Thank you. Do you have an ETA on my transfer?"

She frowned. "I'm sorry, sir, I don't, but we have a room ready for when she arrives."

"Good." He headed for Room 6 and found Leroux sitting up in bed with a nurse checking his dressing, looking none the worse for wear save for the fact his right arm was bandaged up and he was wearing a hospital gown. "How are you feeling, son?"

Leroux shrugged. "Not too bad. I don't know why everyone complains so much about getting shot."

Morrison chuckled. "From what the doctor said, that was a Hollywood wound. Come and see me when you actually have a bullet contact bone. Are you good to work?"

Leroux gingerly tested his arm, wincing slightly. "I wouldn't challenge anyone to an arm wrestle, but if you mean manning my station, absolutely."

"Good. Tell me what happened. Leave out anything that might be classified. This isn't a secure area."

"I have Level Two clearance," said the nurse.

"Nowhere near high enough, I'm afraid."

She finished checking Leroux's bandage. "The doctor said you're clear to leave if you want, but highly recommends you stay in the building or not be alone for the next twenty-four hours. If you feel anything out of the ordinary, get yourself medical attention immediately. There's a remote possibility of internal bleeding." She headed for the door, then turned. "No arm wrestling or push-up competitions."

Leroux chuckled. "You're warning off the wrong guy."

She left the room and Morrison closed the door. "Report."

"I went to visit Sonya at the hospital." Leroux's eyes shot wide. "Did you get it?"

"Yes. What is it?"

"You don't know yet?"

"It's all in Chinese."

"That makes sense. I'm pretty sure it's the intel Dylan was sent to collect. Sonya was careful about what she said, but implied Fang delivered it to her after it was transmitted to Dylan's off-the-books OC."

"So, he's activated that?"

"It would appear so, probably as soon as Sierra Protocol was announced."

"Who's manning it besides Fang?"

"No idea. The list of people he's entrusted with that info I can almost count on one hand. And most of them are either out of the country or in this building."

"So, what happened? She gave you the memory stick, then what?"

"I left, got on the elevator, went down to the parking level, and noticed somebody following me. I ran to my car, got in, but couldn't get the door closed in time. He attacked but I managed to get away. He fired several rounds, caught me in the arm, then began chasing me in his own vehicle before the police got involved. I decided it was best to get to HQ and deal with the paperwork rather than hope a police officer might be able to defend me against a trained enemy operative."

"You definitely made the right choice."

Leroux bolted to his feet. "He got my phone!"

"What?"

"He got my phone. I put it in my shirt pocket, and when he was attacking me, he must have got it because I tried to make a call and the phone wasn't paired, so that means it didn't just fall out inside the car."

Morrison pulled out his phone, dialing his assistant.

"Yes, sir."

"Contact Randy Child in OC-Two. Tell him to trace all activity on Leroux's phone for the past two hours."

"Yes, sir."

Morrison ended the call. "Who knows, we might get lucky. I doubt it, but you never know."

"Sir, if I was attacked at the hospital, it had to be for that intel. How could they know? Who were they following?"

Morrison sighed as he folded his arms, shaking his head slowly. "Any of you, I suppose. Casey knows about you all, has worked with you all, so she could have provided your names to her handler."

"But how would they know about the intel?"

"She was backup last night, so she would have been briefed that Dylan was going in to meet an asset with valuable intel. If I had to hazard a guess, she passed that info on to her handler who perhaps was a little too excited about hearing it and she realized she had probably just killed Dylan. She couldn't live with the guilt so she got in a tub full of hot water and slit her wrists."

Leroux's face clouded at the description. "Yeah, that makes sense. So, she told them she was the backup on the op. She would have told them I was the primary. Then she probably gave them our organizational structure so they would know about Tong. We already know they know about Fang, and probably her relationship with Dylan. If they didn't, she could have told them. You're right, they could have been watching any of us. Wait, do they know about Sierra Protocol?"

Morrison grunted. "It's on the news. The whole damn world knows."

"The world knows about Sierra Protocol, but they don't know what it is. Could they have triggered it intentionally?"

Morrison stepped back and leaned against the wall. "You mean orchestrated this entire thing?"

"Yes. Go with me on this. They find out from Casey that Dylan's heading to China on an urgent op to meet with an asset to collect critical intel. The Chinese suspect what this intel might be and can't risk it getting into our hands, but can't do anything to stop him directly without risking us simply sending in an operative they're not aware of to take his place. They have to let the exchange happen. That way they know for sure whom he's meeting and then retrieve the intel. But the only way they can guarantee the intel doesn't get transmitted is if they cut him off from us. The only way they can do that is to force Sierra Protocol. He loses all his support, and we don't accept any transmissions. They take him down, recover the intel, interrogate him for as long as they can until we lift the protocol and discover he's missing."

Morrison's head bobbed slowly. "I like it, except for one thing."

"What's that?"

"We triggered Sierra Protocol because Casey committed suicide and left a note suggesting there was a leak. How could they possibly know that's how she would react? She could have got on the phone, she could have come in, she could have said nothing. There's no way they could have—" Morrison stopped, his jaw dropping with the sudden realization of how it all could fit. He stared at Leroux. "What if she didn't kill herself?"

Leroux's eyes bulged as he sat back down on the bed. "Holy shit! Of course, it makes perfect sense. It would explain why the timing is just too perfect, it would explain the typewritten note, and it would explain how this is totally out of character." He stood back up. "What if she didn't even know it was happening?"

Morrison pushed off the wall, excited by the possibility. "You mean she didn't know about the briefcase with the transmitter?"

"Exactly. We know it was new two months ago. It could have been a gift. Maybe somebody inserted themselves into her life. Maybe she ordered it off the Internet and it was intercepted and modified. She might have had no idea what was going on. Just by listening in to her conversations, they would know all of our identities except possibly Fang's, and would know about the op, because she would have been briefed about it on her last shift."

Morrison closed his eyes for a moment. "God, I love the sound of that story. It never sat right with me that she was a traitor, but this would explain everything. The key to everything is that damn briefcase."

Leroux stabbed the air with his finger. "Exactly. The briefcase. If we assume she was murdered, that means the murderer was in her house last night. Why didn't he take the case with him?"

Morrison smiled. "Because she followed Agency protocol and secured it in the safe."

"Exactly. If she were in on it, she would have left the briefcase out. She had no idea what was happening, that she was being used."

"But someone was still in her house on a weeknight. There was no sign of a break and entry, no signs of a struggle. She had to have known her assailant."

Leroux gasped at the same time as Morrison did as they both came to the same conclusion. "A boyfriend!" they both said.

"Yes, Sonya mentioned that she had drinks with Avril a couple of weeks ago and spoke of a boyfriend. Things were getting serious. She meets this new guy. He gives her a gift. It's a briefcase, so she naturally replaces her old one with it. Uses it every day to show her commitment to him, her appreciation. He maintains the relationship so that she doesn't toss out the briefcase in anger."

Morrison stepped closer. "And then they find out about Dylan's mission, realize how important it is, then fake her suicide, leaving behind a note that would trigger Sierra Protocol, and Bob's your uncle, they've isolated Dylan, shut down our operations, and tied up the loose end that could potentially identify the agent responsible." He tapped his chin. "But what's their contingency plan?"

Leroux's eyes narrowed. "What do you mean?"

"I mean, let's assume everything we just said is right. They have to let Dylan meet with his contact, which means they have to let the intel be handed off. They wouldn't know where the meet was going to be happening, because he kept that to himself. The briefing did indicate it was to be transmitted from Chan's shop. They would have set up a sting operation to take him down as soon as he arrived there, just in case they couldn't pick him up wherever he met with his contact. They have to have a contingency plan in case he's still able to transmit. But who would he transmit to? With Sierra Protocol enacted, the Agency isn't accepting any communications."

"So, they'd have to know he would transmit to someone else that he trusted if he was given the opportunity. Fang?"

"Or someone like her. Our tacit agreement with the Chinese is that she's not to be touched or interfered with in any way, nor is her family back home. We're quite certain they know about her relationship with Dylan, but a mole we have in Beijing confirmed it's not in Dylan's official record, probably because his file would be looked at so frequently, it could raise uncomfortable questions. It would be only natural that they would expect he would transmit the data to her if he got the chance. Obviously he did since she has it. But then what would she do with it? They would have to know she couldn't risk just sitting on it, since she and Dylan are just as aware that the Chinese know about her and where she is. So they know she'd try to get the data to us."

Leroux continued. "Right. And she couldn't just walk up to the Agency, because that might blow the agreement, so they know she'd try to get it to someone she trusted."

Morrison agreed. "A very short list. If they'd been watching her, they would know that she'd trust Dylan, Sherrie, you, and quite possibly—"

Leroux gasped. "Sonya!"

"Exactly."

"Holy shit!" exclaimed Leroux. "Are we saying that Sonya was shot in a targeted attack?"

Morrison's head slowly shook as this idea percolated. It was outrageous, yet it worked. He began pacing in front of the door. "Their contingency, in case he transmits it, is that he's transmitting it to Fang, outside of the Agency. She then is going to try to get it into our hands by using a trusted contact. Her only trusted contacts in country would be within these walls, so they target Sonya, wounding her. That puts her in the hospital, but alive. That gives Fang a point of contact. Fang comes in, and they know it. They realize this has to be the exchange. You show up to visit her, and because you're happy and healthy, they know she's going to pass it on to you, and you're going to bring it back to the Agency. That's when they jump you to get their hands on it, but they failed."

"What do they do now?"

Morrison shrugged. "They're screwed. The intel is already in our hands and they know it. There's nothing they can do about it now, except try to clean up loose ends."

Leroux cursed. "Sonya!"

"She should already be in the building. I ordered her brought here."

Leroux's shoulders slumped. "Thank God." He flinched. "Fang!"

Kane's Off-the-Books Operations Center

Outside Bethesda, Maryland

Tommy's console beeped indicating a secure message had arrived. Fang leaned forward. "Bring it up."

Tommy opened the message. "Two and three secure."

Fang smiled. "That's good. The Chans have made it back to the safe house. Now we just need to hope the rest of the plan works."

Mai took a sip of her orange juice, having finished cleaning the place top to bottom, front to back. Fang couldn't recall it ever smelling so good in here or appearing so tidy. Kane was by no means a slob, but he was still a man. "Isn't he taking an awful risk?"

Fang regarded the woman naïve to the intelligence world lifestyle. "That's the job. The key is mitigating that risk as much as possible. Right now, the Chinese have two choices. They leave him be at the hotel while they try to figure out what's going on, or they pick him up for interrogation to try to find out the same. If I'm them, if they know what that intel is, there's no way they can risk it getting out of the country, so they'll almost definitely have picked him up. But they have to be careful how they treat him. By picking him up, it means the Americans could retaliate and pick up some Chinese agents. If they treat him too poorly, then they risk the same being done to their agents. Unfortunately, that intel is explosive, and something tells me they're not going to care about how their agents might be treated."

"So they could be torturing him?"

Fang nodded, her chest tightening at the prospect. Every time he went out on a mission, this was a possibility, and she had accepted that fact. She had always known what he was from the day she met him, long before the day she fell in love. Yet it didn't make it any easier, for she knew what her country was capable of. There were no laws that were followed behind the walls of the Ministry of State Security.

Mai leaned forward and took her hand. "Are you all right?"

Fang smiled at her then gave her hand a squeeze. "Yes, I just wish I knew what was going on. My guess is he's in custody and being interrogated. He'll hold out as long as he can to make sure the Chans get away and that the intel gets into CIA hands, but he'll eventually break. Unfortunately, what he doesn't realize is that the intel is already in CIA hands and the Chans are safe, so any suffering is now pointless."

"Can we signal him? Maybe through his watch?" asked Tommy.

"No. He couldn't risk looking at it. It'll be on camera."

"I thought it was some fancy thing that could send pulses into his wrist in different patterns."

Fang groaned. "I forgot about that. You're right. Send him the all-clear signal. He should know what that means." Her phone vibrated in her pocket and she fished it out, her eyes narrowing at the unknown number.

"What is it?" asked Tommy, noticing her hesitation.

"Unknown caller. I'm not sure I should take it."

Tommy waved a hand at their surroundings. "Don't worry, we're shielded. All cellphone signals here are actually transmitted over a secure Internet connection via satellite, then bounced off a random tower in another part of the country. They might trace you, but they'll find you in Wyoming or somewhere."

She took the call. "Hello?"

"Hi, Fang, it's me."

Her shoulders slumped in relief at Leroux's voice. "You had me nervous. What's going on?"

"Are you where I think you are?"

"Wyoming?" There was a pause and she decided humor was probably not appropriate at this time, considering the circumstances. "Yes."

"Is anyone with you?"

"Tommy and Mai."

Leroux cursed. "All right, here's the situation. I visited Sonya. She handed me the intel. I was attacked in the parking garage of the hospital but managed to get away and get back to HQ."

"Are you all right?"

"I was shot, but it was just a graze. We think everything was staged. The suicide, Sonya getting shot, Sierra Protocol, everything. If they knew

214

to jump me, they knew that Sonya had the intel, which means they know you gave it to them. Is there any chance you were followed?"

Fang shot out of her seat, snapping her fingers at Tommy as she spun toward the rear wall with the array of monitors. "Security cameras, now." She pointed at Mai. "Pack our stuff. We're leaving." She returned to the conversation with Leroux. "I took all the usual precautions, but that doesn't mean I wasn't followed. They could have put a tracker on my car. I swept it as soon as I was out of the city, but if it was passive, I could have missed it."

"They've been using burst transmitters here, and we know they're using passive technology and only activating it when they need to. What are the cameras showing?"

Fang's eyes flitted between the various views. "Nothing, but that doesn't mean anything. They could still be getting into position."

"All right. Echo Team is inbound."

"Fifteen minutes out," said a voice in the background.

Leroux repeated what the other man had said. "Echo Team's fifteen minutes out. What do you want to do?"

She continued to monitor the cameras, her trained mind reasoning out the problem. She had to assume Echo Team would be a crack unit from the CIA, as capable as any Chinese unit sent against them. She also had to assume that if they got in her car, the only one available to them, they would be tracked. She could go over the thing bumper to bumper and never find it. But if she didn't, the Chinese could hit them on the road, and there would be nothing they could do about it. She could see only one option. "We're going to hole up here. Tell your people to hurry up because I don't know how long we can hold out."

"All right, good luck."

"Good luck to us all." Fang ended the call.

"What's going on?" asked Tommy, his voice fear-laden.

"Our location might be compromised. There was an attempt made on Chris' life at the hospital. He's fine, don't worry. They're sending something called Echo Team here. They're less than fifteen minutes out. There's a chance I was followed here, or they put a tracker on my car after they saw me meet with Sonya. Either way, the Chinese could be here before Echo Team."

Mai returned with their bags. "We need to get out of here, now!"

Fang shut that down. "No. If there's a tracker on my car, they're just going to follow us. At least in here, we have some protection."

Tommy's face was ashen. "But once they breach, we're screwed, aren't we?"

"Yes." Fang headed for the weapons locker. She tossed body armor to the two civilians and fit her own into place. She held up two Glocks. "Do you want them?" Both shook their heads. "Too bad." She handed them over. "You know how to use them?"

They both nodded. "Unfortunately," said Mai.

"Good. We're going to be up against four, possibly eight people. That's it. Watch on the monitors for a count. If they breach, just keep shooting. But if it looks like you're going to be taken, drop your weapons and lie down on the ground. They might still kill you, but they might let you live. Just tell them whatever they want to know. All they care about is that intel, and it's already in the CIA's hands."

"Are we sure?" asked Mai.

"Leroux just called me, remember? Show them what they want. Let them destroy the system. This place is burned the moment they arrive. They're probably going to want to destroy any copies of the intel before we can share it with anyone else." She holstered two Glocks then grabbed an ammo belt, fitting it in place. She clipped on a knife then grabbed an MP5.

"Where are you going?" asked Tommy as she headed down the corridor.

"I'm not just going to wait here to die. Send that all-clear signal while we still have time. I don't want Dylan suffering because we were too worried about ourselves."

Ministry of State Security Headquarters

Beijing, China

Pan cursed as he stared at the footage for the third time, finding it as impossible to believe as he had the first time, yet there was no denying it. Two different traffic cameras had caught it. The footage clearly showed a man who appeared to be Dylan Kane removing a mask revealing an elderly Chinese man. "Is that who I think it is?"

His subordinate nodded. "Yes, sir. That's Chan Chao."

Pan pinched the bridge of his nose as he squeezed his eyes shut, processing this new bit of information. "Wait a minute, this doesn't make sense. Kane's far taller than Chan."

"Yes, sir, but the officers that found the abandoned vehicle said there were some type of prosthetic limbs that he could have worn to make himself appear taller."

Pan paced across the front of the room as everyone stared at him, waiting for instructions. This was his operation. This was his screw-up.

When their mole had reported that Kane was being sent to Beijing on an emergency op to retrieve extremely valuable intel, he had taken immediate action. Kane was tailed from the airport, but the clever bastard had switched hotel rooms, defeating their prepared surveillance. A parabolic mic had picked him up telling his driver to head to the Forbidden Palace. With intelligence teams all across the city, he had tasked a team already nearby to set up before he arrived.

His team in this building had used the cameras positioned throughout the tourist attraction to begin identifying everyone there, and they had quickly found Duan, a State Security employee who shouldn't be there. He had dispatched a team to the man's home, but also initiated a records search to review everything the man had seen in the several days before he had demanded to meet Kane. And they had found the transcript, a document so shocking, he had immediately isolated the analyst unfortunate enough to have made the discovery.

A further search had found images in their database with Kane and Duan together, the backlog in their facial identification project years long, something he had been complaining about for some time.

Now maybe they would listen and assign more resources. If he was still around to be listened to. If he had known what the intel was, he never would have allowed the exchange, yet how could he have known? Who would have ever believed it?

He pursed his lips. "So, what we're saying is that all this footage we have might actually be Chan and not Kane?"

"I'm afraid so, sir. And it gets worse."

"What do you mean? How could it possibly get worse?"

"It's not just today's footage. We don't know how far back it goes. Kane may have never actually met with Duan. It could have been Chan the entire time."

Pan cursed. He was right. If Chan were wearing these prosthetics that gave him the same height as Kane and a mask that made him appear to be Kane, none of their footage could be trusted. Yet Kane had admitted to meeting with Duan on previous occasions. Could it have been innocent like he said, and the traitor Chan simply took advantage by using Kane's likeness?

He stopped his pacing, turning to the room. "All right, let's entertain the possibility that everything we saw today was Chan and not Kane. Chan in disguise leaves the hotel. Kane's driver said that his voice sounded different. If we believe the driver, then it fits. He's dropped off at the Forbidden Palace. He meets with Duan. Duan hands over the stolen intel, then Chan goes to his shop, most likely to transmit the intel to his handlers at Langley. We take down the shop, he escapes. Meanwhile, the real Kane has gone clubbing. I'm willing to entertain that we could be wrong on this, but how did Chan get detailed enough scans of Kane, who just so happens to know Duan and is a suspected American agent?"

"Maybe Chan's not working for the Americans," suggested his subordinate. "Maybe he's working for someone else like the Russians or British. They frame an American operative, which distracts us while Chan's able to make his escape."

Pan's head slowly bobbed. "I could definitely see the Russians doing that, especially the French, not so much the British. So, Duan, who we know is a traitor, has an innocent friendship with an American that may or may not be an enemy agent. The real handler is Chan, working for someone other than the Americans, who provide him with everything he needs to impersonate Kane, Duan's unwitting friend. They do the handover, which could explain why Duan appears so confused because he doesn't recognize the voice, and we follow the wrong damn man, who ends up escaping because we're looking for the wrong face."

"But we know Kane was here on a mission, don't we?"

"Do we? The recordings from the mole indicate that, yes. It's why this entire operation was triggered. But were they referring to the real Kane or the fake Kane? Could they have been using code, just in case their security was compromised? And if Chan is working for someone else, Kane could be on a completely different mission."

"What are we going to do?"

Pan folded his arms and scratched his cheek. "All right, here's what we're going to do. Keep checking the security cameras and track down Duan and his family. They left the station on foot, so they can't have gone far. He's the leak. It's now plugged, but he needs to be arrested and punished for what he did. Keep tracking Chan. When he and his accomplices abandoned the second vehicle, they must have taken a sewer line or storm drain somewhere, and they couldn't have gone too far. Expand the search radius as far as you need to. Put his photo and all the photos we have out to our officers on the streets and at the airports and railway stations. Get them all loaded in the facial recognition system. If they move, we'll catch them."

"What about the data?"

"Our agent reports that it's likely in the hands of the Americans. Unfortunately, there's nothing we can do about that now, except tie up the loose ends. I want anyone who's seen it dead before the sun rises."

"And Kane?"

Pan chewed his cheek for a moment. "Cut him loose, but I want him followed. He was sent here for a reason, and if it wasn't to meet Duan, it was to meet somebody else who's betrayed our country."

"Isn't it likely that's what he was off doing while we were watching Duan and the fake Kane?"

"Probably, but we might get lucky. And there's still a chance that that actually was Kane and we're being played. The two people that attacked the station and freed Chan's wife physically match the description of Kane and Chan, only their faces don't match. Since we know that at least Chan has access to the mask technology, the two of them could have pulled this off wearing disguises."

He growled. This was all so ridiculous. He had already failed in preventing the intel from reaching the Americans. His career was likely over, and the only thing saving his life was that no one but him and the isolated analyst knew what the intel was. He had to tidy things up as best he could by bringing those responsible to justice.

"Get me a secure channel to our asset at Langley."

Langley, Virginia

"Let me know when you're done."

Nathan ended the call with a press of a button on the steering wheel. Things weren't going according to plan at all. He had failed his adopted country. According to those who had saved him, he had been born in America. His corrupt biological parents had sold him, and a Chinese team had liberated him along with a group of children headed for sexual slavery. The other children had been returned to their parents where possible, but his saviors had thought it best he not return to those who had sold him, for they might just do it again.

Instead, he had been adopted by the people he now thought of as his mother and father, and zealously jumped at the opportunity to serve his new country. He was Chinese in every way except blood, though in his early teens he was sent to a camp where others his age were trained to act American. For over ten years he had trained. He was indistinguishable from any American, but was also a deadly weapon.

And apparently, he was drop-dead gorgeous. Honey traps worked both ways. Most people thought of the sexy female being sent in to seduce the male who had information they needed. But in his case, he was sent in to establish relationships with women within the CIA and pump them for information.

It was the best job in the world.

He was serving his adopted country, helping weaken the corrupt capitalist American regime, and constantly making love to women. All were beautiful to him in their own way. He had been fortunate with Casey. She was gorgeous in all the traditional ways, and a fun companion, but extremely tight-lipped about her work.

She hadn't been the first, she was merely the latest. He never stayed with any one woman for too long. He always found that in fresh relationships at the infatuation stage, rather than the deep love stage, these women were more willing to keep their relationships private and extremely willing to accept his gifts, like the briefcase he had given Casey. With her position, he gathered extremely valuable intel, then through casual conversations over dinner or after a sexual encounter, he drew out names of other people she worked with.

Sonya Tong was one of those names. Gentle prompting over several weeks revealed she was second-in-command of an ops center. And single. A beautiful, easy target to manipulate. Unfortunately, due to a traitor in Beijing, all of his hard work had been burned in less than two days.

Two days ago, when he had reviewed the burst transmissions, he had heard reference to an emergency op where a suspected agent named

Dylan Kane was being sent to Beijing ahead of schedule to meet with a contact who had valuable intel. When he had reported this to his handlers, he hadn't thought much of it. Agents were always being sent in on both sides. Quite often, assets wanted to deliver intel personally rather than transmit it, feeling it was safer. But it was also a way to establish a bond that they thought might merit them special attention should they get in trouble.

Within an hour, a senior investigator named Pan Shiying had contacted him, with a plan to take advantage of his discovery and bring down Kane's network. After making love to Casey, he had sent her into the shower first and logged into her laptop using her password captured on a camera he had planted.

He knew from the recordings that she was backup for the operation, so he had hoped she would have briefing notes. He'd found what he was looking for, but unfortunately, she had caught him. It had meant a rather unceremonious end to their relationship, rather than the more tender one he had planned for her later that night. He had rendered her unconscious with a knockout spray, placed her naked in the tub, then slit her wrists, leaving her to die. He printed off the suicide note, making it just vague enough that her bosses would have suspicions that would trigger Sierra Protocol, leaving Kane stranded without help.

Unfortunately, her briefcase had been locked in her safe and the woman always followed her security protocols, the camera he had hidden in the room unable to catch her entering her code, the keypad always shielded by her hand. The Americans would discover the transmitter, and the methods he had been using to get his information out, so he would figure out a new way to use his women, probably blackmail, photos and video of them together doing unspeakable things.

He had been looking forward to doing just those things with Tong. She would be fun. He loved Chinese women. To him, they were the sexiest, most desirable women he had ever encountered, though the Americanized versions of them weren't as ideal. He preferred those who had spent their entire lives in China and understood the culture he loved. Tong was as American as they came, but she looked the part.

Unfortunately, she had to die. She had seen him, and they would eventually put the pieces together, and he couldn't risk being compromised. He had sabotaged her car so it wouldn't start, then waited through three buses for her to arrive. The circumstances had worked out perfectly with her being unprepared for the bus, and it had allowed him to play the chivalrous stranger, her white knight coming to save her. If she had been prepared, he would have figured out some way to strike up a conversation.

As soon as he had spotted her arriving at the bus stop, he had signaled his accomplice who boarded the bus one stop later and opened fire, playing the crazed gunman. The man was well-trained and the shot to Tong's shoulder was expertly placed. His accomplice was to leave the bus after the performance, then disappear with a generous payment, but that had never actually been the plan. The hired gun was to die all along. The struggle had been planned ahead, except for the final part where he disarmed then shot him.

He had waited for the police and paramedics to arrive as any good citizen would, then left when the cameras showed up. The groundwork laid, he would begin the romance with her, and she would eventually become Casey's replacement inside the Agency, and would also hopefully be a conduit for the intel should Kane get it into the country despite Sierra Protocol being engaged. The plan in Beijing had been to take him down before he could send it, then Tong would merely be used as he had used so many others. But somebody had screwed up and the data had been sent.

After visiting Tong in the hospital, he had set up surveillance, sending photos of everybody to Senior Investigator Pan. Beijing had identified Leroux, which he already knew was her supervisor, but more interestingly, Lee Fang, a traitor living in exile. He had no idea what her connection was to things, but it was too much of a coincidence. Beijing refused to say, which was even more telling. When she had returned a second time, he was positive she was the conduit, the traitor continuing to work against her own people. He had placed a transmitter on her car to see where she was going, but remained behind, for whoever visited Tong next from the Agency would be the one handed the intel.

Unfortunately, this time it was his turn to screw up. Leroux had kept his cool, and rather than panicking, had done exactly what he needed to do to get away. Now the intel was irretrievable, and everything had to be burned to the ground.

Infirmary, CIA Headquarters

Langley, Virginia

Leroux stood by Tong's bed where she was checked over by the doctor. "I'm not going to remove the bandages to double-check things," said the woman. "I'm going to assume they did everything right, but your bandages will be due to be changed later. I want you here first thing in the morning so we can take care of that."

"Yes, Doctor."

"With what's going on around here, I assume you're going to want to work."

"Absolutely."

"Can she?" asked Leroux, concerned about his friend overdoing it.

"She can, but keep that arm in a sling. That means typing with one hand, no matter how much it slows you down. And if you feel anything out of the ordinary, you get down here right away. Understood?"

Tong nodded. "Yes."

The doctor pointed at a nearby wheelchair. "Treat her like a queen. I want her taking it as easy as possible."

"Always, Doctor," said Leroux as he grinned at Tong.

She stood. "Can you hand me my bag?"

Leroux fetched it from the wheelchair and handed it over.

"Now, if you'll excuse me, I'm going to get changed. There's no way I'm going into an ops center in a hospital gown with my butt hanging out."

Leroux grinned then headed for the door. "I'll be in the hallway."

The doctor followed him. "I'll get a nurse to help you."

Leroux stepped into the corridor to find Morrison standing there. "How's she doing?"

"Overdoing it, sir, but the doctor seems to think she'll be fine as long as she takes it easy. I'll keep an eye on her. First sign of any trouble, I'll have her back here."

"Good, do that. She's more important than getting some intel translated."

"I think we should just get this stuff translated then get her back in bed."

Morrison chuckled. "Agreed, but you tell her."

Leroux laughed. "Yeah, you're probably right." The door opened and Tong was wheeled through by the nurse.

"One super spy ready for duty," said the woman.

Tong grunted, gesturing at her arm in a sling. "One super spy with a clipped wing"

"You sure you're up to this?" asked Morrison.

"Absolutely, sir. The sooner we find out what this is all about, the sooner we can get Sierra Protocol lifted and get our people to safety."

"Well, let's put that brilliant mind of yours to work," said Leroux as he took over responsibilities for the wheelchair. "Where are we heading?"

"I've got Randy locked up in OC-Two. He's probably going batshit crazy by now."

Tong giggled. "Just seeing that will be worth getting shot. He's probably dizzy from spinning."

They boarded the elevators in silence, anything they had to discuss far too classified to be overheard, even in this building. Their passes were inspected by the armed guards at the operations center. Morrison opened the door and Child sprang from his seat at the sight of Tong.

"Oh, thank God you're all right!" he cried, rushing down the steps to greet her.

The genuine emotion was touching, and Leroux realized this was probably the first time in the young man's life he had ever experienced something like this where someone close to him had almost died.

"Are you all right?"

Tong smiled up at him. "I will be. Somebody give me a hand out of this chair."

Leroux locked the wheels then helped her up.

"We have to look at the files on a secure workstation," said Child, leading the way. "Oh, and I put a trace on your phone, boss, and it's off. Last ping was at the hospital."

"I figured as much. At least now we know."

Tong made her way up the steps as Leroux walked behind her, both hands out, ready to catch her should she stumble. She was moving slowly, and it was evident she was struggling. This was too much for her. She was weaker than she had thought, lying in bed not nearly as taxing as actual walking. He helped her into the chair behind the workstation and she sighed heavily.

"Okay, that was tougher than I thought it was going to be."

Morrison grunted. "At least you admitted to it. Let's just get this over with so you can get back to bed."

Child leaned over and logged in. Morrison handed him the USB key that had nearly cost Leroux his life, and the young specialist inserted it into the secure reader then brought up the first image.

Tong leaned forward. "So, what do we have here?" She began reading. "Looks like it's a transcript of an interrogation. No wait, it's a debriefing. A man named Lingwei, he's describing a successful operation. Everything went according to plan. The subject was terminated. It was made to appear like he died from natural causes. He was an old man so that was easy. He made it appear like heart failure. He said when he told the victim who had sent him and why, he nearly did have a heart attack."

Morrison leaned closer. "We need names. Who are they talking about? Who died? Who sent them? Why?"

She brought up the next image and continued. "What did you say to him? I told him that the president sent me and was most disappointed with his public criticism of his election to a third term."

"Wait a minute," said Morrison, taking a step back and folding his arms. "Is he saying that the Chinese president sanctioned a kill?"

"It appears so."

Child shrugged. "What's the big deal? It's China. Even our president orders people killed."

Morrison agreed. "This can't be why the Chinese are going ape shit, unless they think this is more than it is. Keep going."

Tong continued to quickly read them the highlights. "There's a little banter. I'll put it all in the transcript. But…wait a minute." She brought up the next file. "Holy shit!"

Everyone leaned forward. "What?" asked Leroux.

She pushed back, her mouth agape.

"What is it?" repeated Leroux.

"The victim, it's former President Jiang."

Leroux gasped. "Are you sure?"

"Absolutely. It says, I'll inform the president personally that former President Jiang died of natural causes. As ordered. Good work."

"This is huge. That's like Biden killing Obama."

Tong continued to open the files. "It says here that this was the second assassination of a former leader and one more is planned. It doesn't say who because someone enters the room and ends the debriefing, shouting about how there's not supposed to be any record of this. That's the end of the transcript. I'll do a formal translation, but before we act on it, I highly recommend we get a second person to go over this. This is too critical for there to be any mistakes."

Morrison agreed. "You're right. How old is this?"

"Ten days."

"Now at least we know why the Chinese didn't want us to see this, and why Dylan's contact was so desperate to get it out of his hands."

"Can we use it?" asked Child. "I mean, we have no way of knowing if this is even genuine."

"No, we don't. However, considering what the Chinese have done to try to get their hands on it, I'd say it is. I have to talk to the director, let her know what's going on, and then brief the president. Sonya, give me a complete translation, word for word. Don't worry, we'll get it reviewed. Chris, we need to know everything that was reported on the recent deaths of the two leaders, and then we need to figure out who the third is that they're going to target. I've got an idea on how we just might be able to use this, assuming the president approves."

"How?" asked Child.

And when Morrison explained his idea, Leroux smiled.

It was perfect.

Ministry of State Security Headquarters

Beijing, China

Kane shook Pan's hand. "I'm glad we were able to straighten things out."

Pan appeared none too pleased. "Misunderstandings occur in China as well as America, though not so often here."

Kane shrugged. "We're all only human." He indicated his suitcases sitting nearby. "Is that all my stuff from the hotel?"

"Yes."

"Do I still have a room there?"

"I don't see why you wouldn't. We didn't check you out."

"And my visa's still valid?"

"Yes."

"My employer's going to want to know if I'm free to return in the future."

"That's beyond my control. I don't issue visas. I guess you'll have to just see what happens."

Kane decided not to push his luck. Xu stumbled into the hallway, disheveled, one eye swollen, his nose bleeding onto a split lip. "What the hell did you do to him?" exclaimed Kane, still playing his role as the naïve insurance investigator.

"He ran into a door."

"A fist-shaped door? This is unacceptable. You can't treat people—"

Pan cut him off. "He is a Chinese citizen and none of your concern. Just be thankful we're releasing him along with you."

Kane glared at the man. "Is his car outside?"

"Yes." Pan held out a set of keys. "I suggest you both leave now before I change my mind."

Kane took the keys and stuck them in his pocket. He grabbed his suitcases then headed for the door as Xu shuffled along behind him. They stepped outside and Kane reached into his pocket, pressing the button to unlock Xu's SUV. Lights flashed to his left and he hurried over, popping the rear and putting his luggage inside. He closed the hatch then helped Xu into the passenger seat.

"I'll be doing the driving."

Xu grunted. "You'll get no argument from me."

Kane climbed into the driver's seat and started the engine. "Hospital or home?"

"Home."

Kane activated the GPS. "Put your address in."

Xu complied. "I just want you to know I didn't—"

Kane cut him off before he said something incriminating. "Hey, don't worry about it. What happened was my fault. Case of mistaken identity.

You just sit there and relax. Fall asleep if you want. I'll have you home in it looks like twenty minutes." He could tell from Xu's eyes that he understood. There was no way this vehicle wasn't bugged. The safe haven from earlier was now gone. The question now was what to do? He had received the all-clear signal on his watch. The pulse pattern indicated it had come from his ops center, which meant it was from Fang and the others. The all-clear had to mean that Chan and his wife had signaled they were safe. They must have thought he was being tortured and were letting him know there was no need to suffer any longer. Fortunately, it hadn't come to that, the trick with the mask and the prosthetics having apparently worked. The fact he hadn't received any other communications on his watch suggested Sierra Protocol was still in place.

For now, he had to get Xu back to his family then return to the hotel, doing exactly as the Chinese would expect him to do. He had no doubt the SUV was bugged, and his luggage likely was as well. The hotel was absolutely bugged now, beyond the standard fare, and they would have a massive surveillance team assigned to him, including satellite, drone, and physical. There was no way he was evading them without help.

This mission was over until Sierra Protocol was lifted.

All he could do now was what his cover would, and return on his already scheduled flight. That was all well and good for him. His mission had succeeded in that the intel was now in American hands, but Duan and his family were out there somewhere in desperate need of help, and Chan and his wife were still trapped in a country that now knew they were traitors. He had to fulfill his promise to the old couple. He had to get them out.

The question was, how the hell was he accomplishing that when he was under surveillance and Sierra Protocol was still in force?

Pioneer Internet Cafe

Beijing, China

Duan sat behind the keyboard in the Internet cafe. His family was in an alleyway out back, but he didn't know how much longer they could evade the authorities. He had followed the instructions Kane had once given him should something like this happen.

Get underground.

Literally.

There was an underpass near the police station they had escaped from, and they had entered a storm sewer. There would be no cameras. Unfortunately, his granddaughter was terrified and began screaming uncontrollably, which had forced them back to the surface, though a good distance from the station. He was to contact Kane through a coded website, but without his phone, he didn't have Internet access, which had forced him in here.

He typed in the URL, memorized long ago but never visited, and a travel website, much like the one he had been recruited through, appeared. He clicked the travel agent login link, entered his code, and was presented with a text box. He quickly described the situation, begging for help, and indicating he didn't have access to the Internet but had bought a new phone. He entered the number then closed the browser and hurried out of the shop and down the alleyway. The sun was breaking now, and it would soon be daylight.

Beijing was about to wake up, and then there would be no hope for them.

Please, Kane, help us.

Chan's Safe House

Beijing, China

Chan kneeled in front of his wife, gently cleaning her wounds while she held an ice pack to the opposite side of her face. "How are you feeling?"

"Like the entire People's Liberation Army marched on my face."

He chuckled. "Don't worry, you're still beautiful."

"If you think this is beautiful, then you're a far sicker man than I thought you were."

"A far sicker man who loves you."

She grunted. "That's just because you're too old and lazy to find someone else."

He leaned in and gave her a gentle peck on her swollen lips. "I'd never be able to find another one like you. You're one in a million."

"In a country of over a billion."

He continued working. "You really are pessimistic when you're in pain."

"Speaking of pain, I thought you said you had some good painkillers."

"I do, but they're going to mess with your mind, and I don't know when we might have to leave here. It could be minutes, it could be days."

"You're sure they can't track us here?"

"Not completely, so the sooner we get into the CIA's underground railroad, the better. But we should be good here for at least a few hours. If we need to, we have our escape route." Chan's computer beeped, indicating a message. "I have to check that." His wife nodded and he rose, heading over to the machine.

It was a message from Kane's people at his secret operations center, relaying a message from Duan, the contact that had provided Kane with the intel. He was in trouble and needed help. Chan sighed. There would be no help coming from the Americans, and the message indicated Duan was with his children and grandchildren. Kane probably had a similar arrangement with this man, like he had with him and Bing to get them out if they got in trouble.

He hadn't heard from Kane, which meant the man had likely been picked up at the hotel and was being tortured right now. He glanced over at his wife, gently pressing the ice pack to her lips and wincing. He didn't want to leave her, but right now, he might be the only hope for these poor souls. He fired back a message with a burner phone number, then rejoined his wife.

"I'm going to have to leave."

She stared up at him through the narrow slits of her swollen eyes. "Why?"

"Kane's contact, Duan. He and his family are in trouble. I have to go get them. Will you be all right here alone?"

"I think so. Just get me in the bed. I want to sleep now."

He helped her up and then into the bed, covering her with a blanket. He put a bottle of water and Tylenol beside her, and a burner phone. He took a knee beside her, taking her hand in his, gently brushing the hair from her face, his heart breaking. "I'm going to give you the good painkillers."

She smiled slightly. "I knew my husband loved me."

He pulled the bottle from his pocket, placing two of the pills in her mouth. He held the bottle up to her lips, and she took a drink, swallowing the pills. "You'll be feeling those soon." He put the bottle beside her. "Don't take any more for at least four hours. I should be back long before that, though."

She reached up and ran her hand down his cheek, staring into his eyes. "Do you forgive me, Husband?"

His chest ached. "Forgive you for what?"

"For being such a difficult woman to live with."

He smiled at her and took her hand, kissing it, then pressing it to his chin. "There's nothing to forgive, my love. Every minute of every day spent with you was perfect, and I wouldn't change a thing."

She smiled, tears flowing. "I'm going to go to sleep now. You go save those children. I love you, Husband," she said, her voice fading away as she drifted off.

He kissed her forehead. "And I love you, too."

Her chest collapsed as she exhaled slowly, and his heart pounded. He checked for a pulse but found none. "No!" he screamed, leaning back and staring up at the heavens through clenched eyes. He collapsed atop her, holding her lifeless body tight against him, sobbing uncontrollably. His precious wife was gone, his reason for living extinguished, beaten to death by those they had fought together their entire lives. He climbed into bed beside her and wrapped his arms around her, holding her tight against him.

Then reached for the bottle of painkillers, all will to live gone.

Hotel Hilton Beijing Wangfujing

Beijing, China

Kane lathered up his kibbles and bits and surrounding areas for a second time, just to make sure he hadn't missed any remains from his earlier performance. He had dropped Xu off at his family home, triggering a panic within the household and a verbal assault from his sister.

"What happened to him?" Xu's sister, the source of the cheap perfume, had asked.

"I was jumped outside a nightclub and your brother saved me." He dropped a massive wad of bills in her hand. "Anything he needs, use that. If you need more, he knows how to reach me."

He left the young man with his family, taking the SUV back to the hotel where Xu could collect it later. The young man was roughed up but not in any danger, perhaps half a dozen blows to the face and none to the body. If Xu had recollected his interrogation correctly, he should be fine. Kane had no doubt his driver had stuck to his story, and the fact they had let them both go suggested the Chinese had enough doubt that they didn't know what to think. A passive scan of his hotel room indicated at least half a dozen new signals, including some high-intensity ones that suggested video surveillance. There was no video in the shower, so he took the opportunity to check his messages.

He read the plea from Duan and the reply from Chan. He suppressed a curse. Chan had done enough. His place was at Bing's side. Duan was Kane's responsibility, the CIA's responsibility, but with this damn Sierra Protocol in place, there wasn't much they could do. He sent a message through his encrypted app to be relayed to the burner phone Chan had indicated Duan should contact.

I'm out and at the hotel. Status?

He waited but there was no reply, and it had him nervous. He turned off the water and stepped out of the shower, grabbing a towel off the rack. The phone vibrated with a message and he checked it.

Bing is dead.

Kane's heart broke and he bit down on a knuckle as he leaned his forehead against the tile wall opposite the camera hidden behind the mirror. Tears flowed, not only for the woman he had known for years, but for her husband and his friend, now all alone in this world. He feared what his friend would do now that his reason to live was lost. He thought of Casey's suicide and how her betrayal had cost so much already.

People were dead, families destroyed, years of work torn asunder.

And he feared that was only the beginning.

Kane's Off-the-Books Operations Center

Outside Bethesda, Maryland

Fang activated her comms, foregoing proper communications protocols. It might just confuse Tommy. Their transmissions were encrypted, so any hostiles wouldn't get anything useful out of it regardless. "Tommy, it's Fang, report."

"Nothing on the cameras yet."

"Check the road camera."

"Just a second." Tommy cursed. "There are two SUVs parked on the side of the road."

"Anybody in them?"

"Not that I can see."

"Reverse the footage."

"Hold on."

She could hear him working his station. "Okay, wait, I've got it. They arrived together. Four people got out of each of them, so eight in total."

"Weapons?"

"I'm not really good with that stuff, but it looks like they all have machine guns of some type."

"Understood. Contact Chris. Let him know there are eight hostiles with assault rifles."

"On it. Are you going to be okay? Maybe it's better if you get in here with us."

She headed toward the rear of the storage yard. "How many minutes ago did they arrive?"

"Four."

"Good, then they're still positioning themselves at the rear." She sprinted down the side of a container, coming to a halt at the end, checking to make sure she was still clear. "And Tommy?"

"Yes?"

"If I don't make it, tell Dylan—"

"You're going to make it."

"I know, I know, but just in case, tell him that I love him, and that he gave me a life better than I could have ever imagined. You tell him that, all right?"

Tommy's reply was subdued. "I will."

"Good. Now keep your eyes out for any movement and report it to me by direction from where you are with numbers. The road is south. Don't be surprised if I don't reply, I might be keeping radio silence. Understood?"

"Yes, ma'am."

"Good. Going silent." She sprinted across to the next container, heading for the trees at the back of the compound. If she were running the op, she'd have sent one team to the back, through the trees surrounding the lot, since she wouldn't know where the cameras were placed. It meant she had a brief window of opportunity where their attackers would assume they had the element of surprise as they rushed into position so they didn't delay the first team.

She reached the final container, the fence line only feet away, thick trees on the other side. She cupped a hand around her ear and listened. Twigs snapped and branches swayed to her immediate left as at least one person barged through the underbrush. She slung her MP5 and drew her Glock, twisting a suppressor in place. Something moved just to her left and a figure emerged, grabbing the fence. There was more movement in the trees and a second figure appeared. The first was already halfway up the fence. She put two rounds in his chest, then two more in his friend, both dropping. Gunfire rang out to her right and she rolled back behind the container, sprinting down the side, falling back two rows before cutting over.

"Are you all right? We're hearing gunfire."

"Two down. They spotted me. Anything on camera?"

"Not yet. Wait a minute. Rear fence line, two guys climbing over. And two are now at your car."

"Understood. Keep an eye out for the other two. I don't want them sneaking up on me. Going silent." She sprinted across from west to east toward where her car was parked. The two at the rear fence line would be checking on their friends, which meant they'd be heading in the opposite direction. It bought her perhaps two minutes, since they would be careful about it. If she could take out the two at her car, it would halve the number she was facing. It would also halve the number from each team, which would mean the four remaining wouldn't be accustomed to working together. It would weaken their effectiveness, though only slightly. These would be highly trained professionals, though out of practice, sleeper teams like this rarely seeing action once assigned.

She, on the other hand, had been Special Forces in regular rotation, seeing action all across the globe, and probably had more experience than the average team combined. Her concern at the moment was the two missing hostiles. The terrain didn't offer a high point for an overseer position, though snipers could be put on top of one of the containers, or perhaps even in the trees.

She skidded to a halt, checking to make sure she was still clear. "Watch for movement on top of the containers. And if you have any view of the trees, check for a sniper up in them."

"Copy that," replied Tommy. "We're not seeing anything yet. The two guys at the back are checking on the two you took out. The other two are just leaving your car now, heading toward us."

"Copy that. Going silent." Her car was just ahead. This could be her last chance for an easy kill.

"I see you," said Tommy in her ear. "The two guys from the parking lot are coming up along the side of the container just ahead of you to your right."

She gave a thumbs-up signal and raced across, taking up position at the corner of another container that would give her a wider angle. She took a knee, her weapon extended in front of her.

"First one is about to come around the corner, second one is right behind him."

She spotted the first and held her fire. She needed both of them. The second one emerged. She squeezed the trigger, hitting him twice, taking the second target out so he couldn't duck back behind cover, then fired two more at the first one as he spun toward her. He collapsed and she rushed forward, tapping both in the head before ducking behind the nearest container.

She pressed against the side, steadying her breathing, listening for any sign of the missing two hostiles. A shot rang out and something slammed into her back, dropping her to the ground, and as she struggled to remain conscious, she opened her mouth to apologize to Tommy and Mai for failing them.

But no words came.

"Oh my God!" cried Mai as she leaped from her seat and rushed forward, squinting at the screen. "Is she all right?"

Tommy's chest was tight as his heart slammed. He had heard the shot, even through the insulated walls of the container. It was some sort of high-powered weapon. He zoomed in on Fang's prone figure, searching for any signs of life, but saw nothing. Something moving out of the corner of his eye caught his attention, and he stared at the surface of his coffee as it rippled. He placed his palm flat on the desktop. Vibrations.

"What is it?" asked Mai.

"I can feel vibrations."

"What do you think it is?"

He reached forward and flicked a switch, turning on the external audio. And smiled. "It's a helicopter! It must be Echo Team!"

Tanner fired and smiled as the Chinese sniper dropped from his perch in the tree, the infrared scanners having easily picked him out as they approached. "Control, Echo-One. I've taken out one target. Do we have an update from the friendlies, over?"

"Stand by, patching you through."

"Hello?"

"Is this Tommy?"

"Yes, ma'am."

"I'm Tanner, Echo Team leader. We're arriving by chopper. Report."

"Fang's just been shot."

Curses erupted from the team.

"Understood. I need a report on the hostiles. How many did you take out?"

"Four. There are two at the rear that are heading toward our position now and two we can't see."

"Understood. We're inserting now. Stay inside until you hear from me, and keep your eyes open on those cameras. I took out one in the trees. Probably one of your missing two, but there are still others out there."

"Yes, ma'am."

The chopper touched down on the roadway and Tanner hopped out with the rest of her team. Sprinting into the storage yard, she sent them off in twos as she scanned from left to right, searching for any movement.

A shot rang out and Carlos Sanchez grunted, dropping to the ground beside her. She cursed and dropped to her knee, noting Sanchez had taken a round to his upper left arm and dropped straight, giving her a line on the source. "We've got a shooter near the road at the west end of the lot!" She grabbed Sanchez by the collar and hauled him to his feet. He groaned in agony as they stumbled for cover. Gunfire erupted to her left, several MP5s opening up. She reached the nearest container and pushed Sanchez against it, helping him to a seated position.

"Holy shit, that hurts."

"It's supposed to, idiot. That's why most of us avoid getting shot."

"I thought I was doing a good job by making sure you were taking point."

She yanked his med kit off his belt and pulled out the tourniquet.

"Why the hell did he shoot me and not you? You were in the lead."

Tanner shrugged as she tied the tourniquet above the wound, stemming the flow of blood. "I make a smaller target. Maybe he's not a very good shot and didn't want to take the chance." She yanked on the knot and Sanchez gasped.

"I think you got it tight enough."

"You better hope so." She activated her comms. "Control, Echo-One. Sanchez took a round to the arm. Have medevac standing by, over."

"Copy that, Echo-One. Notifying local emergency responders. We'll instruct them to hold back until you give the all-clear."

"Copy that, Control." She shoved Sanchez's weapon back in his hands. "You good to fight?"

"I'm good. Don't you worry about me."

"I never do." Tanner shot to her feet and rushed to the end of the container, gunfire still rattling from the west end of the compound. "Echo Team, report."

"We're pinned down, southwest corner," replied Lyons.

What sounded like HKs had joined into the fray, her team now engaged by at least two, if not three hostiles. "Tommy, this is Tanner. Tell me where the bad guys are."

"Judging from where your guys are firing, I think one is in the trees at the west end of the compound near the road. The other two are on either side of the container near the west end. If you continue forward past the next row of containers, you should have a clear shot all the way across the lot and you should be able to take them by surprise."

"Good thinking, kid. You tell me if they move." She sprinted across the gap between the two rows of containers then continued to the next. She checked to make sure there were no surprises, then raced as fast as she could as some of the guns fell silent.

"Hostile in the trees taken out," reported Lyons. "Two more still have us pinned down, over."

"Copy that, Echo-Two. I'm coming to save your asses yet again."

Lyons chuckled. "Well, can you hurry it up, please? I've got dinner plans."

The rattle from the Chinese position continued to grow louder and she eased up, not wanting to risk her footfalls being overheard should someone stop firing to reload. She readied her weapon as she came to the corner of the container. She peered around, spotting the hostile. She fired two rounds into his back and he collapsed to his knees. She put one in his head to make sure he was finished.

His partner continued to fire on the opposite side of the container. He let up for a brief moment, no doubt listening for what had happened to his friend. She couldn't give him time to think. She darted across the back of the last container between her and the enemy, and came around the corner, her finger on the trigger, ready to fire. Someone grabbed the barrel of her weapon, yanking it forward, her along with it. As she was swung by her assailant, she reached up with her left hand and grabbed him by the vest, dragging him down with her. She yanked her knife off her belt with her right hand as they hit the ground with him on his back and her straddling. Her hand darted forward, shoving the six-inch blade under his vest and into his ribcage, piercing his heart. His eyes shot wide as she twisted, a gush of warm blood soaking her hand as the entire area fell silent.

She pulled her knife free and stood over her kill, staring down at the light fading from the man's eyes. This one she would remember. She activated her comms. "Consider your asses saved. Do a complete sweep of the area. Make sure there aren't any others, over."

"Copy that, Echo-One," replied Lyons. She cleaned her knife on the man's pant leg then sheathed it before wiping her hand off as well as best she could.

"Tommy, this is Tanner. We believe we've eliminated all the hostiles. Can you confirm that you don't see anything?"

"No, just your people. You have to check on Fang."

"Where is she?"

"From your position, one row closer to the road, then down about half a dozen containers on your right. You can't miss her. I'm coming out."

"No, stay where you are. Wait until we secure the area." Tanner jogged down the row of containers. "Sanchez, you still with us?"

"Of course I am. You know my social life. I've got nowhere better to be."

She spotted Fang lying face down beside a container. She knelt beside her and checked her over, finding a round embedded in her body armor. "Are you okay?"

Fang groaned. "Do I look okay?"

Tanner gripped the bullet then wiggled it free, confirming it hadn't gone all the way through. "You're lucky. Looks like he hit you at an angle. Your body armor did its job."

"My body armor did a job on my shoulder. I'm pretty sure something's broken. Might be my shoulder blade."

"It could be, but you're alive. Do you think you can stand?"

"Anything's better than the mouthful of dirt I'm now enjoying."

Tanner chuckled. "Let's see if we can get you up without causing you to pass out."

"Passing out once in one day is more than enough for me. The kids still holed up?"

"They're fine. We've eliminated all the hostiles. Can you confirm there were eight?"

"Yeah, that's all we saw arriving. The number fits Chinese protocols. Two four-man sleeper cells." Fang gasped as Tanner hauled her to her feet. "I forgot what it feels like to get shot."

Tanner grinned. "I try to avoid it myself. Now, why don't you show me to this highly illegal operations center one of our officers has? I'm imagining a James Bond lair."

Fang gingerly led her down a row of containers. "Then, my dear, you're going to be very disappointed."

Tommy and Mai hugged each other, ecstatic that Fang was alive. He pressed the button, unlocking the front door as she arrived with whom he assumed was Tanner. He and Mai rushed down the corridor and Mai gasped at the agony on Fang's face.

"Oh no, are you all right?"

"I will be."

"We should get you in one of the beds."

"No time for that. Just get me to the control station."

Tanner and Tommy helped her into the control room and into one of the chairs. Fang leaned forward and pressed her thumb on the Control key before tapping Escape five times. A prompt appeared and she tapped the Y key then was prompted again to type the word YES. She did and hit enter. All the screens went blank.

"What's happening?" asked Tommy.

"Basically, a digital self-destruct." Fang extended a hand to Tanner who pulled her up. "We've got about two minutes to get out of here before that digital self-destruct is done and the real self-destruct starts."

Tanner cursed as they headed for the corridor and the door to safety. She activated her comms. "Echo Team, Echo-One. Everybody get to the road, now. And somebody pick up Sanchez, over."

"This is Echo-Two, I've got him," replied Lyons. "Heading for the road now."

Mai was the last out with their bags, and Fang jerked her chin at the container. "Close the door."

Tommy shoved it shut, wondering if he'd ever work here again.

"Let's get going," urged Tanner. They all rushed toward the road as the chopper thundered overhead, sirens approaching in the distance. They reached the road just as the helicopter landed. "My orders are to bring you all to headquarters until the situation's resolved. We have medical facilities there, but if you want to go with the locals, you can. Sanchez will be going with them."

Fang waved off the offer. "I'll tough it out."

"Yeah, nuts to that," said Sanchez, grimacing.

Tanner gave him a look. "Don't be a hero. You're bleeding pretty good there, even with the tourniquet. Let the locals deal with it. Mike, you stay with him."

"Yes, ma'am. Always happy to babysit the idiot who gets himself shot."

Sanchez gave him the stink eye. "It's not like I invited it."

Tanner motioned toward their ride. "All right, everybody else in the chopper. I don't want to be here when the locals arrive. Mike, you know what to tell them."

"I'm a well-trained lackey, don't you worry."

"That's the spirit." Two of Echo Team helped Fang into the back of the chopper and moments later they were lifting off.

Tommy peered out the window to see a string of police cars and several ambulances winding their way along the road approaching the lot. He squinted down at the containers then his eyes bulged. "I don't think the self-destruct worked! I don't see any explosions. It has to have been two minutes."

Fang shook her head. "It's not that type of self-destruct. It's completely internal. As soon as the digital wipe completes, several different chemicals stored in the ceiling are triggered to mix and then spray over every surface. It'll melt everything in there. Any DNA, fingerprints, clothing, paper, plastic, motherboards, storage devices. When it's done, there'll be nothing left for anyone to make sense of."

"Sounds expensive," said Tanner. "I hope your friend's got good insurance."

Fang laughed. "Something tells me State Farm doesn't have secret lair insurance."

Mai leaned forward. "What about Dylan? Isn't he cut off now?"

"When I initiated the self-destruct, it automatically sent out a message to certain people. If he doesn't know, he'll know the next time he checks in."

"So, he's on his own?"

"Yes, until Sierra Protocol is lifted, then the CIA will have his back."

Tanner frowned. "Yeah, until they abandon him again."

Chan's Safe House

Beijing, China

Chan stared at the bottle gripped in his hand then down at his wife. This is not what she would have wanted. She would have wanted him to go on, to continue the work, and right now there was a family out there that needed his help, and if he took the easy way out of his misery, they were as good as dead.

He hurled the pills across the room then stared into the still face of his beloved wife, gutted that his final memory of her would be this. He ran his fingers across her cheek. "Goodbye, my love."

He climbed out of the bed then tucked in her blanket. He stepped back, gazing down at her. If he didn't know better, she was merely sleeping. He closed his eyes and said a silent prayer, hoping against hope the Christians were right and there was an afterlife where she would be waiting for him to be together forever, finally free of this oppressive regime.

He sent a message to Kane's phone from his burner.

Going to pick them up now.

Operations Center 2, CIA Headquarters

Langley, Virginia

Leroux rose as Morrison entered the room followed by Therrien and the rest of the team. "Sierra Protocol has just been lifted and all operations centers including backups are being brought online until we've heard from every one of our assets." Morrison jerked his chin toward the displays, the operation at Kane's set up outside Bethesda having been monitored by satellite though they hadn't participated. "Status?"

"Eight presumed Chinese hostiles eliminated. Fang took a round to the shoulder but her body armor absorbed the impact. She might have some broken bones but the latest report is that she thinks it's just deep bruising. Tommy and Mai are secure. One Echo Team member took a round to his arm and is being treated by locals. The chopper is inbound now. ETA Ten minutes."

"And our friend's little setup?"

"Literally liquidated, sir."

Morrison chuckled. "Something tells me there's a lot of high-stakes poker in his future."

"Why's that?" asked Child.

"I'll explain it to you later." Leroux turned to Morrison. "So, what did the director think of your idea?"

"She loved it. She's running it up to the president now. Assuming he approves, we'll move forward with it, but right now, I want every one of my officers and assets notified that Sierra Protocol has been lifted. Your team will be focusing on Kane and the operation there. Everyone else will be getting things back online."

"Yes, sir."

Morrison turned to Tong. "How are you holding up?"

Leroux didn't want to say anything, but she looked terrible, weak. "She's pushing herself too hard."

"I'll be all right, sir."

Morrison frowned. "I think you should go to the infirmary."

"No, sir. I'm just tired, that's all."

Morrison sighed. "Fine. Let's see what's going on with Kane. If he's secure, get some rest."

"Yes, sir."

Morrison left and Leroux sat at his station then sent the all-clear signal to Kane's watch, the coded pulse surreptitiously signaling to his friend that Sierra Protocol had been lifted, just in case he was surrounded by the enemy.

He just prayed his friend's watch wasn't sending the pulses into the wrist of a corpse.

Hotel Hilton Beijing Wangfujing

Beijing, China

Kane lay on the bed, as frustrated as he could ever remember with all the surveillance on him. There was nothing to do but watch the television and surf the Internet or play a game of 2048 on his phone. He had just received a message from Chan indicating he was heading out to pick up Duan and his family. It was a high-risk operation and he wished he could help, but that was impossible. The surveillance on him would be so thick now it would block out the stars. He was stuck here until Sierra Protocol was lifted and they could find a way to get him out.

His watch pulsed a coded sequence indicating it was from Langley, and he suppressed a smile. It meant Sierra Protocol was lifted. He headed for the toilet and dropped his pants, parking himself on the throne, already aware that the camera in the bathroom was at the wrong angle to see his screen from this position. He quickly fired an update to what he assumed was Leroux.

I'm secure at my hotel. Room 407. Heavy electronic surveillance inside room. Chan Chao is en route to pick up Duan and his family. Assist as best as possible. Chan Bing is dead. Will require exfil for Duan family and Chao. Contact Beijing Station. I need to get out of this room as quickly as possible. Need surveillance defeated and two faces. Me and whoever delivers it so we can exchange positions.

He received a response a moment later.

Copy that. Your OC was compromised. Fang initiated liquidation protocol. Fang, Tommy, and Mai are en route to HQ with Echo Team. Sierra Protocol lifted. We're back online.

Kane closed the secure app and leaned back on the toilet, closing his eyes, saying a silent prayer for Chan. He shouldn't be doing this alone. He wasn't in the right frame of mind to be on an op by himself.

Operations Center 2, CIA Headquarters

Langley, Virginia

Leroux exchanged a relieved smile with Tong, elated to hear that Kane was still alive. But he wasn't out of trouble yet, and by the sounds of his message, he intended to get into more. Leroux turned to Child. "Can we book the room above or below him? Ideally above."

"Just a sec." Child worked his magic and a few moments later kicked off a victory spin. "The hotel reservation system shows that the room above him is vacant."

"Book it." Leroux turned to Therrien. "Contact Beijing Station. Tell them we need a team to override the surveillance in his room and we need someone to swap places, so matching faces and clothing."

"I'm on it."

Leroux's terminal beeped with a private message. He brought it up, dropping back into his chair as he read the update from his girlfriend Sherrie.

I'm all right and safe. Looking forward to seeing you soon. Love you, Sherrie.

He typed a quick reply.

So happy to hear you're okay. See you soon. Love you.

The message showed as received and he leaned back, noticing Tong staring at him.

"What's up?" she asked.

"Just heard from Sherrie. She's all right."

"That's good news. I know you've been worried."

"You have no idea. How are you feeling? Do you want to go get some rest? I think we can handle things here."

Tong dismissed the suggestion. "Not until our people are safe. This is all going down in the next hour or two. I can last. Don't worry about me. Let's just get our people home."

Beijing, China

Chan's phone rang as he headed toward the last recorded position of the Duan family. He answered the call, putting it on speaker. "Hello?"

"Hello, this is Duan Guofeng."

Chan cursed. "No names, you fool! Where are you?"

"We're in an alleyway behind—"

"Wait, can you describe where you are without giving specific locations?"

"We're still in the alleyway behind where I sent the message."

"Understood. I'll be there in five minutes. Is it wide enough for me to back in?"

"Yes, it is."

Chan grabbed the tablet off the passenger seat, the map already zoomed in on the area where the Internet cafe was. "I'm going to come in from the west end. As soon as you see me, you open the rear door and get everyone inside. Before you do, get rid of everything you've got.

Phones, tablets, laptops, watches, jewelry, jackets, bags, everything. Empty your pockets. Any piece of clothing, anything that wasn't always in your sight when you were arrested. Gone. I don't care if I've got a bunch of naked people getting in here with me. If they put a tracker on one of you, this is all over. Understood?"

"Yes, sir." Duan's voice trembled, suggesting he did indeed get it.

"Good. When I hang up, you turn off that phone, crush it with your shoe, and be ready. I'm four minutes out. I'll see you soon."

Chan ended the call then turned his phone off. Duan had said his name and there was a chance his government might have recorded the conversation. The Chinese had their own version of Echelon, though it wasn't as advanced, but it was getting there. There was no privacy in China, and he found it laughable how huge TikTok had become worldwide. Every single piece of data that someone shared on TikTok was data the Chinese government could access. By law. It didn't matter if the servers weren't within Chinese borders, all that mattered was that if the government demanded access to the data on servers in America, the Chinese citizens behind the company had to grant access, or they were dead, despite any assurances to the contrary.

Keep dancing, teenagers of America.

The Chinese government is watching.

Behind the Pioneer Internet Cafe

Beijing, China

Duan crushed the phone under his foot and his wife gasped. "Why did you do that?"

"Because he told me to."

"Should you go buy another?"

"No, he's going to be here in less than four minutes." He turned to his family. "Drop your bags. Take off your jackets. Any electronics, watches, jewelry, everything on the ground. Now!" He took his own jacket off and tossed it aside. "Empty your pockets, everything. They might have planted a tracker on us." The instructions were reluctantly followed. "If you're wearing anything or have anything that wasn't in your sight the entire time since the authorities showed up at the apartment, get rid of it."

Everybody looked at each other, but nothing else was dropped.

"Good." He checked his watch then grinned at his bare wrist. "Oops!" The children giggled. "All right, he's going to be coming from that end of the alleyway." He pointed. "Let's get down there. As soon as he arrives, we all get in. We stay quiet. I'm the only one who does any talking." An engine revved and he spotted a van pulling past the alleyway before backing in. "Let's go. Quickly."

They all rushed forward and Duan opened the back doors to find an old man in the driver's seat, looking back at him.

"Get in. Stay down. Stay quiet."

Duan lifted the children into the back then helped his wife, his daughters' husbands helping them.

"Hey, what's going on there?" shouted someone from down the alley.

"Ignore him," ordered the driver. Duan climbed in then reached out, shutting the doors. The engine revved and he tumbled backward, his sons-in-law catching him and helping him to a seated position. The driver looked over his shoulder and cursed. "How many are you?"

"Nine."

He cursed again. The children giggled. "I hope they can handle nine."

Duan tensed. "What do you mean?"

"It doesn't matter. It's too late now. Just stay down and keep your mouths shut no matter what happens. We'll be there in about fifteen minutes."

Duan lay down on the floor, holding his wife against him, his own body joining in her trembling, wondering if they were finally safe.

Operations Center 2, CIA Headquarters

Langley, Virginia

The door to the operations center hissed open and Leroux looked up to see Morrison entering, then was shocked to see him followed by Fang, Tommy, and Mai.

"Holy shit! Cool!" exclaimed Tommy, his eyes wide, his mouth agape as he took in the spectacle of a fully manned operations center in the middle of an op.

Morrison headed for Leroux's workstation and Leroux rose. "Status?"

"Sir, all OCs are up and running and all priority officers are being contacted. The acknowledgments are starting to roll in from around the world. It looks like no one was taken but we've ordered all our China officers to stay underground until we can see if they were exposed after we review our own voice logs of Avril's shifts. It's going to take time, but we'll figure out the exact extent of the breach eventually."

"What about Dylan?"

"He's in his hotel. Beijing Station is moving into position to tap his bugs and they're sending in someone to do a switch so he can get out and help Chao. Chao's picking up the Duan family."

"Good. Any idea where he'll take them?"

"None, and we're limiting contact because we don't know the extent of any monitoring that might have been set up. Our best guess is he's taking them to wherever he was already holed up."

Fang cleared her throat and stepped forward. "It's a converted garage. I have the exact address on my phone." She pulled it out and read it off.

Leroux jerked his chin at Tong. "Bring that up, would you?"

Fang handed her phone over to Tong who brought up a satellite image of the area.

"Great. Now, we have a starting point. Let's prep an exfil plan to get them all out and into the underground railroad. If we're lucky, they'll all be out within a few days and Dylan can just leave on his return flight with no one the wiser."

Child grunted. "You're assuming everything goes as planned. Nothing has so far."

Chan's Safe House

Beijing, China

Chan pulled into the garage then pressed the button to close the door behind them. He turned off the engine and twisted in his seat. "We're here. Everybody out the back but stay quiet." He climbed out and the back door of the van opened. He walked over to the door to the inner sanctuary and stepped through, half-expecting Bing to greet him. He turned to the others filing in behind him. "Just find a place to sit. Not the bed, my wife's..." He paused. "Sleeping." He headed for his terminal and sent a message to Kane's secure system but it came back with a rejection. He scanned through his messages and frowned when he saw an automated one indicating the system was being taken offline permanently due to a breach. Something was obviously wrong, though he had another message here indicating that Sierra Protocol had been lifted. At least it meant he could communicate securely with Langley.

He sent them a message.

I have Duan family. I need to exfil immediately. Nine souls.

He could send a message from his burner phone to Kane but decided against it now that there was a secure method of communication available. Once again, the machine beeped with a message from Langley.

Acknowledged. Stand by.

He leaned back, folding his arms. "What the hell else am I going to do?"

Hotel Hilton Beijing Wangfujing

Beijing, China

Kane sat on the toilet, staring at his phone as if he were reading something, not moving a muscle, timing his blinking on a 3-4-2 count. A message appeared on his screen.

We've got it. Knock, knock.

A moment later there was a knock at the door. He rose, wiped needlessly from habit, and flushed, then washed his hands and headed to the door. "Who is it?"

"I have a delivery for Dylan Kane of Shaw's of London."

He opened the door and smiled. "Come in, there'll be a reply." He closed the door then pointed at the couch. "Have a seat. You caught me in the middle of something. Sorry, I drank too much last night."

The messenger sat and Kane headed back into the bathroom and sat on the toilet, pulling his phone out and recreating what he had just done a moment ago. Another message silently came in.

You're looped. Make it quick.

Kane stripped down to his underwear then headed back into the other room. "We're on a loop."

The messenger rose, chuckling. "I hope so. I'm open-minded but I don't swing on that side of the vine."

Kane laughed as the operative from Beijing Station opened his messenger satchel. He handed Kane a mask and a set of clothes. Kane quickly donned the outfit that exactly matched the messenger, but to his size, while the messenger put Kane's clothes on and then his own mask. Kane helped him adjust it, the effect of staring into his own face unsettling.

"How do I look?" asked the messenger.

"Gorgeous, but apparently that's wasted on you."

The man laughed as he then adjusted Kane's mask. "It's like looking in a mirror."

Kane jerked a thumb over his shoulder. "Bathroom. Pants and gitch around your ankles, knees spread, phone in your right hand."

The messenger headed to the bathroom as Kane continued to adjust his clothing. Everything had to appear as if it fit properly and hadn't been hastily put on. He stepped over to the bathroom and peeked through the door.

"You look good. Three-four-two on the blinking."

"Gotcha."

Kane closed the door and headed for the couch, grabbing the satchel before sitting where the messenger had sat. "End the loop," he said aloud. After a few seconds, the toilet flushed and the messenger appeared. Kane rose, handing him an envelope.

The messenger opened the envelope then read what it said and frowned. "Never mind, there won't be a reply right now. I'll contact you when I'm ready."

Kane nodded then left the hotel room, leaving his doppelganger to play his part. He rode down the elevator in silence then headed outside, spotting the courier vehicle parked nearby, its hazards flashing. He climbed in and pulled away, and once he was on the road, he reached into the glove compartment and retrieved the comms waiting for him. He fit the earpiece in place and activated it.

"Control, Goodtime Boy. I'm baaaack."

Operations Center 2, CIA Headquarters

Langley, Virginia

Cheers erupted from everyone in the operations center at Kane's voice echoing over the speakers. It was one thing to get a message. Messages could be faked, messages could be forced, but Kane being Kane meant he was fine.

"Good to have you back, Goodtime Boy. What's your status?"

"I've made the switch and I'm in the courier vehicle now. I'm going to the exchange point, then I'm going to go help Chao. What's the status there?"

"A lot's been happening, but I'll give you a quick update. Fang, Tommy, and Mai are here at the OC with me. They were forced to do a shutdown of your location. It was compromised by the Chinese."

"Understood. I'll deal with that when I get home. I'm just happy everyone's safe. How's Sonya doing?"

Leroux nodded at Tong who jacked into the conversation.

"I'm fine, Dylan. Thanks."

"How's that shoulder?"

"Better than I expected. Chris got shot too."

Chris gave her a look. "Just a graze. Nothing like hers."

Kane laughed. "We'll all get naked and compare scars when I get home."

Tong giggled and Leroux flushed. "Yeah, I think I'll pass on that one, buddy."

"What's the status on Chao?"

"He's returned to his secure location with the Duans."

"Status on the exfil?"

"In progress. We're just getting everything back up and running around here, so it's going to take a little longer than usual to get them onto the railroad."

"Any indication the Chinese know?"

Leroux glanced at the satellite footage showing the area. "Negative. So far, we're seeing no unusual activity."

"Understood. Let's hope that security problem you had is actually plugged."

McLean, Virginia

Nathan smiled as another burst transmission arrived, the operations center door obviously having opened once again. He retrieved the file and ran it through the AI translator, pulling a rough transcript of everything picked up, clicking on key points in the file to listen to the actual words spoken.

And he chuckled.

These Americans are just too trusting.

Senior Investigator Pan's career might be over, but if the intel he had just gathered were acted upon quickly enough, the man's life might just be saved.

He sent a message to Pan.

I've found Chan and Duan.

Operations Center 2, CIA Headquarters

Langley, Virginia

Everyone spun toward the door as Neary burst into the operations center, followed by half a dozen heavily armed security personnel and several people carrying scanners, all spreading across the front of the room, their weapons aimed at Leroux's team. Leroux shot to his feet. "What the hell's going on here?"

Neary shut the door. "We detected a burst transmission a few minutes ago. Nobody moves."

Leroux stepped forward. "Lower your damn weapons."

The guards hesitated until Neary gestured for them to stand down.

"Good." Leroux turned to the room. "Everyone back away from your terminals. Let them do their job."

Neary waved a finger at the workstations. "Tear this place apart. We need to find that transmitter."

Leroux growled. "Bullshit, just open the damn door again."

"No, it will transmit what's just happened and whoever is receiving the signal will know we've found them out."

Leroux shook his head. "No. The analysis of the briefcase showed it wouldn't transmit more than once every fifteen minutes, but it will react to the stray signals. If you just received a burst transmission, then there won't be another one if you open it now."

Neary paused as he considered Leroux's suggestion, then stepped back over to the door and opened it.

"Got it." A woman holding a scanner swept the detector in front of her, homing in on the signal. She slowly climbed the steps toward Leroux's station then swung to the right. Tong gasped as she pushed back in her chair, the scanner beeping rapidly, the frequency increasing as the detector neared the bag she had brought from the hospital.

Neary rushed forward and unzipped the bag, yanking things out. "I knew it was too soon to lift Sierra Protocol. If we had waited three full shifts like I wanted, we would have detected this without any harm being done."

Leroux stepped over to Tong's station. "You don't seriously think she's a mole, do you?"

"No, but something in her bag was transmitting." He tipped the bag up to make certain it was empty and handed it to the woman with the scanner. She ran her wand over it.

"It's not the bag."

Neary pointed at the contents now sitting on Tong's workstation. "Identify anything you don't recognize."

Tong had watched every item taken from the bag and shook her head. "I recognize everything." Her jaw dropped and her eyes bulged as she grabbed the teddy bear. "Nathan!"

En Route to Chan's Safe House

Beijing, China

Kane floored it with Leroux's last message. The CIA had been compromised again. This was ridiculous. "Does that mean you're about to enact Sierra Protocol again?"

"Negative, the Chief says the leak's been plugged but a transmission was definitely sent about five minutes ago."

"Is there any sign Chao's position has been compromised?"

"Not yet, but we've got what appears to be about a dozen emergency vehicles heading into that area. It could just be a coincidence."

"I don't believe in them. How far out?"

"Five, maybe six minutes."

"Okay. I'm pulling up there now. I want reports every sixty seconds."

"You've got it."

Kane parked the car and hopped out. He sprinted to the side door and knocked 3-1-2, then opened it. He stepped through the garage, the van to his left, then entered the converted sanctuary area. Everyone gasped and Kane pointed at his face. "It's just a mask. Duan, it's me, Dylan."

Duan stared at him, puzzled, but Kane had no time to convince him. Chan was sitting on the edge of the bed holding Bing's hand, and it took Kane a moment to remember the woman was dead.

"We've got to go now. Everybody in the van."

Nobody moved. He jerked a thumb over his shoulder. "Now! The authorities are on their way. Less than five minutes."

Duan leaped to his feet as did the other adults, herding the children toward the door.

Kane walked over to Chan. "Let's go, buddy."

Chan shook his head. "I'm not leaving."

"What do you mean?"

"I can't leave her, not like this." A tear rolled down the old man's cheek.

Kane took a knee beside him. "You realize what they'll do to you?"

Chan stared into his eyes. "I'll never give them the chance. Now just go. I'll buy you time."

"Four minutes," reported Leroux.

There was no point nor any time to argue. Kane reached out and squeezed the man by the shoulder. "It's been an honor and a privilege. You and Bing will be remembered."

Chan bowed his head for a moment then met Kane's gaze once again. "Just tell me one thing."

"What's that?"

"Was it worth it?"

"Was the intel worth it?" Kane smiled. "From what I've been told, with what they have planned, your wife won't have died in vain."

"Good. Now go."

Kane patted Chan's shoulder one last time then jogged out of the room and hopped into the driver's seat. He pressed the opener clipped to the visor and the garage door rolled open behind him as he started the engine. He pulled out, closing it again before shifting into drive and flooring it. He activated his comms. "Give me a location."

Leroux replied immediately. "Sending the coordinates to your phone now."

Kane pulled his phone out of his pocket as he made a right turn. He brought up the message and tapped on the coordinates, a map appearing. He handed the phone back to Duan. "You navigate."

Chan rose and headed to a cabinet at the back of the room and opened it. He pulled out body armor and strapped it in place, then put on a second set loosely over the first. He flipped the table onto its side meant for just this situation, the top reinforced. He loaded and lay every weapon he had on the floor behind the table, then took a knee as tires screeched outside. He fit a pair of ballistic goggles over his eyes, noise protectors in his ears, then a helmet over his head.

An explosion from the far end of the converted garage indicated they had blown the door to the outside. He grabbed a Type 80 assault rifle and readied himself. Orders were shouted and the soles of boots pounded on the concrete as the assault team surged inside. He glanced over at his beloved. "I'll be with you soon, my wife."

A soldier appeared in full gear. Chan squeezed the trigger, several rounds erupting from the weapon, the sound deafening in the confined space, the recoil painful. He knew how to use these weapons, he knew how to shoot, but he rarely got the opportunity to actually practice. Despite that, the man dropped. Chan swung his weapon from left to right, holding the trigger in, firing round after round through the thin wall. Several cries were heard from the other side, then something clattered on the floor. He spotted a flashbang and ducked, squeezing his eyes shut.

The grenade exploded, the din still deafening through his ear protection. He popped back up and continued to fire. The weapon clicked and he tossed it aside, grabbing the next one, resuming his assault on those behind the wall. An engine roared followed by a massive crashing sound. This was it. He rose to his feet, continuing to fire blindly, a roar erupting. "This is for the great Chan Bing who died for freedom!"

The wall between the garage and his sanctuary splintered then pushed apart toward him. He inhaled sharply at the sight of an armored vehicle racing through the rubble at him. He continued to fire uselessly, the rounds pinging off the armored plating as they continued to surge toward him. It slammed into the table he had been using as cover then into him, carrying him back to the far concrete wall. He cried out in agony as his pelvis was crushed between the wall and the unforgiving front of the police vehicle. His head slumped to the side and he noticed the bed, with his wife still on it, had been pushed along as well. The armored car backed up and he collapsed to the floor, and with his last bit of strength, he dragged himself toward her, draping himself over her lifeless body.

"I love you, my wife."

Duan pointed between the seats from the rear. "Just up here on the right."

Kane pulled the van over and two men who appeared local jumped out of a delivery truck. Kane pointed as the rear doors were opened. "Everybody goes now. Get inside the back of that truck."

Duan looked at him. "Do you trust these people?"

"With my life. You'll be fine. As soon as you're in that truck, you're in the underground railroad. We use it all the time. It works. You'll be in America in a few days. Just do what they say, no hesitations." Kane climbed out as the Duan family piled out of the back of the van and rushed into the waiting delivery truck. He walked up to one of the men. "Keys."

A set of keys were tossed over to him and the man pointed across the street at another vehicle that matched the one the messenger had arrived in. Kane headed directly over, saying nothing else to the Duan family, and started the car as the delivery truck pulled away, on its way to its first exchange point. Once the Duans were in the next segment of the underground railroad, the likelihood of them safely escaping the country was almost assured.

Kane activated his comms. "What's the status on Chao?"

Leroux's response was subdued. "I'm sorry to report that he's almost definitely dead from what we saw."

"Understood. At least now he's with his wife."

If you believe in that sort of thing.

Beijing Capital International Airport

Beijing, China

Kane sat at the gate, waiting for his flight, eager to get out of a country he actually enjoyed being in. Chan Chao and Bing were dead, confirmed when the two body bags were brought out and caught on satellite. He would miss them. They were good people. Honorable, trustworthy, but more importantly, they were his friends and they would be mourned.

He had paid a courtesy call to Xu earlier today, returning the man's SUV, just as would have been expected by the character he played. The man was fine, he had a good shiner and a swollen lip, but unlike poor Bing, he had survived. Now Kane just wanted to get home, to hold his girlfriend and spend time with his friends, as they all healed, everyone torn apart by what had happened.

He muttered a curse as Pan came around the corner. Kane rose, getting back into character. "Mr. Pan. Are you here to stop me from leaving?"

Pan shook his head. "No, Mr. Kane, I'm just making sure you actually leave. Have you heard from Duan?"

"No, and I'm guessing after what happened, I won't. Why? Have you not found him?"

"No."

Kane regarded the man. "If I say I'm not disappointed to hear that, will I still be allowed to leave?"

Pan chuckled. "Mr. Kane, it's been interesting. We both know who you are, but you played the game well. If I'm not punished for my failure, I look forward to our next encounter."

Kane extended his hand as they announced boarding for his flight had begun. "Let's hope you invite me to a better venue next time. Perhaps you could be my new friend since Duan has disappeared."

Pan laughed. "You do have an interesting sense of humor." He pointed at the gate. "Your flight is boarding. Leave our country, and pray you don't cross my path again, Mr. Kane."

The Union Restaurant

McLean, Virginia

Tong sat at a table facing the door. Her heart raced and her shoulder throbbed, though the doctors assured her she was recovering well. It had been three days since Kane had successfully made it out of China. The moment she had realized the betrayal, Leroux had activated the lockdown, sealing the door so no one accidentally opened it. The transmitter had been found inside the teddy bear. It hadn't been scanned when she arrived with Echo Team. Neary disabled the power source, then in a shielded room, they wiped everything recorded since the last transmission, hiding the fact the device had been discovered.

She had carried on the budding romance through text messages, then arranged this lunch. Her comms squawked in her ear, Leroux on the other end.

"Someone just arrived matching the description you provided. He's handsome. Nice ass."

She giggled. "Stop, you'll make me blow my cover."

"Sorry. He's coming through the door now."

She spotted Nathan and her heart ached. The first man she thought had liked her in a very long time had been a fake. He never liked her. He was using her from the beginning. He had left her heartbroken, convinced once again she was doomed to die alone.

And it pissed her off.

Nathan smiled at her, clearly unaware of what was about to happen to him. She rose, the signal that this was indeed him, and the entire restaurant stood along with her, weapons drawn, all aimed at Nathan. Her would-be lover bolted for the door, driving a palm into the nose of the first agent in his way, delivering a kick to the chest to the next. More agents burst through the front door and he spun around, making eye contact with her.

He growled, sprinting toward her, shoving his way past the agents scrambling to stop him. Nobody was opening fire. They wanted him alive, they wanted him for interrogation, but she wasn't willing to get hurt again because of this maniac. She drew her weapon and fired twice, center mass, just as she had been trained, and the man whom she thought might be her savior gripped at his chest before collapsing mere feet from her. She stepped over to him as he gasped, staring up at her.

"Tell me one thing."

"What?"

"Did Avril know?"

Nathan smiled. "She was as ignorant as you." His hand suddenly whipped out from behind him, gripping a weapon, and she fired two more rounds into him.

"That's for Avril, you piece of shit."

His lip curled. "All you did was stick a finger in the dyke."

Operations Center 2, CIA Headquarters

Langley, Virginia

Kane stood in the middle of the operations center, his hands on his hips as he stared at the massive display curving across the front of the room, the culmination of all their efforts, all their suffering, about to hopefully pay off. Duan and his family were safe, having made it to the US last week. He had made contact with them but likely would never see them again. They were receiving training in how to assimilate into their new lives, and would be given new identities where they would hopefully spend the rest of their days in peace.

His own operations center was literally liquefied. Because it was so well disguised, the local authorities had never found it when they came to investigate the shooting, and they weren't prying any further since it was classified as a national security operation. Once things had cooled down, he had sent in subcontractors to remove his two containers. They were now crushed into cubes, perhaps already recycled, the rest of the supporting equipment woven through the surrounding area removed by different contractors. He had already reached out to his contacts and a new operations center was being built. It would take some time, but he was looking forward to it.

New was always better.

"There he is," said Tong, pointing.

Kane and the room stared at the displays, showing a live feed from the Chinese Communist Party Policy Convention. Duan's intel had been delivered to Hu Jintao, the third target on the list, able to go into hiding thanks to everyone who had sacrificed so much. The old man descended from the rear of the room, slowly making his way deeper into the chamber, occupied by over one thousand members of the Chinese Communist Party. The room fell silent as the man not seen since being escorted out of the previous gathering reached the podium then stood behind the lectern. He adjusted the microphone.

"This is it," murmured Leroux.

"I'm here to commemorate Jiang Zemin and Bao Tong, and if I hadn't received what you're about to see, you would all be commemorating my death as well."

Kane smiled, grabbing Leroux by the shoulder and giving him a shake as the transcript appeared on the large screen behind the elderly man, voice actors recreating the conversation, the transcript along with the original screenshots synced to the audio as it progressed. The chamber became agitated, men leaping to their feet, demanding an explanation.

And then the president rose, his lips pressed together so tightly they were merely thin lines. He walked out with his entourage as the entire chamber stood, shouting at him, demanding the truth, a truth Kane had no doubt would never come. He could only hope that the damage done to the Chinese president was enough to bring change to the Communist regime, and perhaps take them one step closer to the dream of a democratic China that his good friends had died for.

Rest in peace, my friends. I hope it was all worth it.

THE END

ACKNOWLEDGMENTS

Some might wonder why I would dedicate a book to someone who committed suicide. The Christian belief is that suicide is the ultimate sin, but this is 2022, and most now realize that mental illness is a real thing and should be spoken of.

Ask yourself, has someone in your life changed? Do you no longer hear from them? I disappeared for years. I was the life of the party for a decade, then dropped off the map with all my medical issues.

And almost no one asked why.

Because we still have this aversion to discussing our health, especially mental health.

It's difficult. Even I hid everything I was going through, but now I'm writing these words in the hopes that someone who might be going through something similar reaches for the phone rather than a bottle of pills.

Make that call.

People love you, even if you think you're all alone and abandoned by the ones you thought cared.

When I needed help after suffering a medical crisis all alone during COVID, my friends came through. They drove me to appointments that were over an hour away, they picked me up, they shopped for me. All I needed to do was ask.

You can't blame people for not helping when they don't know you need help.

Make that call.

The scene at the beginning of this novel where Avril Casey believes she committed suicide was written around the same time news broke of tWitch's death, which prompted the dedication, and this plea.

As usual, there are people to thank. Brent Richards for some weapons info, my dad for all the research, and, as always, my wife, daughter, my late mother who will always be an angel on my shoulder as I write, as well as my friends for their continued support, and my fantastic proofreading team!

To those who have not already done so, please visit my website at www.jrobertkennedy.com, then sign up for the Insider's Club to be notified of new book releases. Your email address will never be shared or sold.

Thank you once again for reading.

Made in United States
Orlando, FL
14 January 2023

28669884R00186